2021 EU Prize for Literature Jury Statement on The River

The River by Laura Vinogradova is a fine combination of the great writing tradition of many Latvian women writers and of a deep and very personal exploration of serious topics that almost all women face in their daily lives. Vinogradova's work is based on a proper and thorough understanding of composition and structure, and on a great ability to express, in rather spare prose, eternal emotions and longings for nature, for history, for human relationships. Vinogradova entered the Latvian literary scene in 2017. In 2018, her first collection of stories, *izelpas* (*exhalations*), gained the attention of critics and readers, and the publication of her novel *The River* in 2020 has brought her a nomination in the Best Prose Book category for the Annual Latvian Literature Award 2020. The publishers describe the book as very touching, emotionally rich and of high literary quality, while the Annual Latvian Literature Award jury describes *The River* as "a microworld . . . a present into which the long shadows of the past stretch, a psychological and melancholic story about loneliness and longing, a mosaic of lost moments coloured with hope for the future."

THE RIVER

by Laura Vinogradova

Translated by Kaija Straumanis

Curated by Kaija Straumanis as part of the 2025 Translator Triptych

OPEN LETTER
LITERARY TRANSLATIONS FROM THE UNIVERSITY OF ROCHESTER

Originally published in Latvian as *Upe* by Zvaigzne ABC, 2020
Copyright © Laura Vinogradova, 2020
Copyright © Apgāds Zvaigzne ABC, 2020
Translation copyright © Kaija Straumanis, 2025

First edition, 2025
All rights reserved.

Library of Congress Control Number: 2024952469
ISBN (pb): 978-1-960385-13-0 | ISBN (ebook): 978-1-960385-20-8

This project is supported in part by an award from the National Endowment for the Arts.

This project is also made possible by the New York State Council on the Arts with the support of the Office of the Governor and the New York State Legislature.

Cover design by Jenny Volvovski
Illustrations © Vasilijs Vinogradovs

Published by Open Letter at the University of Rochester
Morey 303, Rochester, NY 14627
www.openletterbooks.org

Printed on permanent/durable acid-free paper.

THE RIVER

BEFORE

Dina likes Rute's place. There's a warmth to it, the sort of warmth that's oblivious to the weather outside. As soon as she steps into her sister's apartment, Dina takes off her boots and socks and stands for some time, barefoot, soaking up the warmth. Rute has heated floors; Rute has everything.

—What are you doing? Rute laughs.

—Have you been outside?

—No, I've been working. What is it?

—The wind, little sister, the wind.

—There's wind in here, too, Rute laughs again and blows air into Dina's face.

They drink coffee. Rute orders a pizza. Dina's eyes wander around the kitchen; hungrily taking in every beautiful detail, because Rute's space is beautiful. Warm and beautiful. Sometimes Dina wants to call her out on it, tell her she's spoiled, tell her Stefans spoils her. Because Dina can't escape—not the cold, not her loneliness. And sometimes she feels like she can't even try. Can't be free of it, doesn't deserve to be. And then she gets angry at Rute. Angry because Rute shouldn't be living in an apartment like this, shouldn't have heated floors, or love, shouldn't be stringing fairy lights from all the shelves.

Rute has a jar of kombucha fermenting on the windowsill. When Dina sees it, she chokes on her coffee and wheezes while laughing.

—What's that? she points to the jar.

—Kombucha.

—Why is there lace over the top of it?, still laughing.

Rute pouts and says nothing.

—It reminds me of something. Dina grows thoughtful.

—Kombucha? Rute's voice drips with sarcasm.

But Dina shakes her head. The pizza is delivered. The sisters eat, their fingers greasy, and forget about the kombucha.

—Walk me out? Dina asks, but Rute shakes her head.

—I want to get a bit more translating done.

They hug each other tightly; Rute blows Dina a kiss, and the door closes behind her.

After that, everything happens too fast to make sense of it. Too fast to scream, too forcefully to fight back. Dina gets off the No. 6 tram at the Mārkalne stop and heads for home. The street is quiet and empty, with a few cold cars and a red mini-van parked along the side of the street. It's a snowless, windy January, and Dina retreats deeper into her scarf. It all happens in a second: three men jump out of a van, grab her, pull a bag over her head. They lift her like a ragdoll and toss her into the back of the van. No shouting, no reflexive attempt to escape.

Dina freezes and gives in because at some point in her life she stopped fighting back.

She lies silent in the back of the van and tries to think. Is she hurt? Will she survive this? Will it be quick? But she can't think clearly. Her goddamn mind is trapped in this bag. Everything is trapped, even her fear. She doesn't feel afraid. What she feels are her pants, wet and cold, plastered to her skin. She's pissed herself. They seem to have left the city because the road is straight, smooth, and fast. Dina is curled up into a ball, lying in her own urine, with a bag over her head. Suddenly, she realizes what Rute's kombucha reminded her of.

At the time, Dina would have been around ten years old. One day, without a word, their mother had taken her and Rute to live with Aigars. No, we're not going back home, their mother had told the girls, and they never brought it up again. Their mother loved Aigars just as much as she'd loved Vladimir before him, and Igor before him, and Jānis somewhere in between. Aigars wasn't bad, he left the girls alone. He never spoke to them, and the girls quickly learned to do the same. If they talked or laughed, it meant a black eye for their mother. But she loved Aigars even with her black eye, so the girls weren't worried.

The sisters didn't have their own room at first, instead sharing one with their mother and Aigars. They were set up on the floor behind the armoire, with a quilt for a mattress and a small nightlight. But it was still dark. Each night, Dina had to listen to their mother's panting and snoring, and Aigars's moaning. Dina and Rute wet their "bed" on the very first night. Dina had been embarrassed to tell their mother, but worked up the courage and finally did. The girls were given a clean sheet, but the same thing happened the next night and the night after that. Dina would wake up to a wet quilt and a sheet with a large yellow stain on it. She pulled on her jeans and went to school, but felt that damp cold on her legs the entire day. This time she didn't tell their mother—they didn't have that many clean sheets, and their mother was busy. Aigars wanted to spend every second with her. He didn't like it when she wanted to play with Dina and Rute.

The girls spent several months sleeping behind the armoire, wetting the bed every night. Sometimes they couldn't tell if it had been Dina, Rute, or both of them. They'd study the stains on the sheets, trying to make sense of it, but what did it matter? Either way, the bed was wet. Either way, it stank. Either way, they had to sleep there again. Every morning Dina would pull back the sheet, hoping it would be the last time, that everything would dry out and she wouldn't wet the bed anymore. But she did, and so did Rute.

Then they got their own room, and while moving them in, their mother saw their sleeping space for the first time. She saw the piss-stained sheets, the cotton quilt they'd used as a mattress, starting to mold. Their mother said nothing; neither did the girls. Urine isn't something you talk about.

Having their own room was better. They each had their own bed and were given special mattress covers. Dina's bed stayed dry the first few nights, and she was happy because she thought she'd overcome bed-wetting. There was one morning when Rute's bed was damp, but she was still little. She couldn't hold it in.

One night, Dina woke up needing to pee. But the toilet was outside, and she'd have to pass Aigars's room to get to it. What if she woke him and he got angry? What if he took it out on their mother? Because sometimes he did that when he got angry. And at those times it seemed that their mother didn't love him after all—but that wasn't true. She did love him. She'd cry, rub ointment on her bruises, and go on loving him.

Dina got an idea. On the table was a jar used for rinsing paint brushes. She'd pee in there. She squatted, positioned the jar under herself, and tried to aim in the dark. She filled the jar to the top, a bit of warm urine dripping onto her hands. But Dina was pleased. Her bed would stay dry, she wouldn't go to school smelly. She found a few more jars in the courtyard and secretly stashed them in their room. She filled those, too. When she ran out of jars, she peed into a vase that was kept in the girls' room because Aigars didn't like vases. And when she ran out of vases, she peed in the bowl that sat under the flowerpot.

On rare occasions she would take the jars outside to empty them. Very rarely. And so, the urine-filled jars would turn dark, cloudy. Like—jars of kombucha. Now she remembers.

The van stops and Dina is dragged outside. Through the bag she can feel the damp sea air. She recognizes it because Vladimir, whom her mother had loved, had lived by the sea. The sea air makes up a part of her childhood air. We all start at childhood. She takes a deep breath of this air and savors it. Then comes a sharp pain on the back of her head, then darkness.

CHAPTER 1

Rute sits on a small stool in front of the stove, her head resting between her knees and her hands submerged in a bowl of warm water. She's washing dishes, slowly and clumsily. She's used to having a dishwasher, and the plates slip out of her hands, the forks prick her fingers. She sets the clean dishes on the floor next to the stool. Then she picks up the bowl of water, now full of coffee grounds and bits of food, to dump it outside behind the house. She opens the door carefully, the full bowl in her hands, and stops, startled: a young woman is in the yard, a little boy stands at her side and another child kicking in her stomach. Rute doesn't see this, but can sense it. The woman's coat is fastened only over her breasts, her stomach stronger than the buttons, splitting the coat in two.

For a moment the two women look at each other. The boy is tightly holding his mother's hand. Rute thinks, *Why isn't he wearing mittens? It's still cold.*

—Hi! the woman says. We live next door.

Rute is silent.

—I saw a light in the windows yesterday. We came to see if everything was alright.

Rute is still silent, the bowl of water still in her hands, one foot holding the door open.

—I'm Matilde, and this is Lūkass, the woman says and nods at the boy. We live over there.

Rute turns to look at the distant house. She can only make out the roof; the house itself is obscured by the old shed and leafless bushes.

Lūkass tries to pull away from Matilde's grasp, but she holds him tight.

—Rute, Rute finally says her own name.

—Are you old Jūle's daughter? Matilde is not shy.

—Yes.

—I thought so, right away. You remind me of him. The younger one? He had two kids right? That's what he told us.

—Yes.

—You never came around . . . Matilde trails off.

Rute doesn't reply, and Matilde looks uncomfortable.

—Well, we'll see you. She puts a hand on her large stomach.

The other hand holds Lūkass's. They turn and leave. Rute is still standing with the bowl of water in her hands. At the gate, Matilde looks back at her.

—If you need anything . . .

Rute nods. Matilde waits another second, in case Rute says anything more, but no. Then Lūkass carefully pushes the gate shut and reaches for his mother. Matilde lifts him up and settles him above her stomach, his muddy boots dirtying her coat.

Rute dries the dishes with an old towel and thinks about this Matilde. She's never seen red hair quite like hers. Well, dyed, sure, but Matilde's is natural. And such large eyes and teeth. Rute thinks that, back in the city, women would do something about teeth that big. Suffer through braces, file and shape them. But Matilde lives here, by the river. Here even big teeth can be beautiful. And maybe her teeth don't even matter because she has those huge eyes. Stare into eyes like that and who cares how big her teeth are. Matilde is small and petite, except her stomach, which is like a balloon about to burst. You wouldn't want to touch it for fear of it popping. How can Matilde manage such a large stomach? And carry Lūkass on top of it? She's slender and strong. *Just like Mom*, Rute thinks.

Then she takes a bucket and goes down to the river. It's right there, very close. Just a few paces away. The old dock is rotting but sturdy. The spring runoff almost covers it, and the riverbank is lined with dried reeds. Rute stares into the depths of the water for some time. There's darkness there. Darkness and a mirror. She sees herself in it, sees her winter, her northern blood. She lifts her hand and brings it to her hair. It's as gray as a wool blanket. And Rute thinks again of Matilde. Imagines herself with Matilde's red hair.

That night she wakes to the sound of someone knocking on the door, loud and insistent. Rute lies silent, but then the knocking moves to her window.

—Rute! she hears Matilde calling. Open up! Please!

Rute gets up, throws an old jacket over her shoulders, and opens the door. Matilde is there with Lūkass. Rute turns on the light, and the sleepy Lūkass shields his eyes with one hand. Matilde pushes him into the house.

—Rute, it's the baby, she says, her voice very calm. Things are moving a little quicker than expected. But it'll be alright, don't worry! she says and guides Lūkass further into the room.

—My ride to the hospital is already on its way. Look after him, okay? Kristofs isn't home yet, but I let him know, he should be here soon, here's my number. Her words tumble and tumble. Rute is as dazed as Lūkass, unable to get a word in.

Matilde crouches next to Lūkass and takes off his jacket. Then she hugs him tightly and plants a kiss on his head. Rute can see the pain in Matilde's large eyes. She's keeping it together for Lūkass, Rute understands that. The boy whimpers.

—You stay here, Mamma has to go to the doctor, okay? I'll be home soon, Matilde promises and her large eyes find Rute's. Okay? she asks, and Rute simply nods, confused.

And then Matilde is gone. Rute stands alone with Lūkass, who cries and runs to the door. She catches the little body and awkwardly pulls it to her own.

—Come on! You can sleep in my bed, okay? she whispers. Sleep, and when you wake your mom will be home.

—I want Mamma, I want Mamma! Lūkass wails and pulls away from Rute, a stranger.

He cries for a long time, but eventually calms down. Rute puts him in her bed and tucks him in.

—I'm going to sit right here, okay? she asks, and Lūkass nods.

—Sing! he says, but she doesn't know how.

—Sing! he demands, and she tries.

Some sort of long-forgotten melody without lyrics. *Mm-m-m-mmmm . . .*

Lūkass falls asleep, but Rute remains sitting. She doesn't want to disturb the boy by lying down next to him, but it's the only bed. Jūle, her father, had lived here alone, and the house is basically empty. Emptier than the houses of other old people. As she sits in the dark listening to Lūkass breathing, Rute wonders: who was Jūle? What kind of person had her father been?

Dina!

Know what I realized? You can't escape other people. Even if you hide away in a deep cave, eventually they'll find you. And there's absolutely no way to hide in a house. I've only been here for five days, and they—other people—already found me. And now I'm sitting next to Lūkass and watching over him as he sleeps. Shit. I don't know anything about kids!

People gravitate toward one another. Seek. Find. Sniff each other out.

They finally turned the electricity back on yesterday. No one out here is in a hurry. Nothing is. Not even the river.

Sis, I miss you. You'd like it here.

CHAPTER 2

Kristofs sees the seagulls even when he's asleep. At times he can hear them despite being far, far away. They're always with him; he hears them in the shower and they tear at him in his dreams.

This morning he wakes from one such cry. He looks at his phone.

—Guuuh . . . he groans and gets to his feet.

The men are probably already waiting for him at the warehouse, while he, the kid, dozes away. Another day of suffering the baby jokes slung at him.

Kristofs hurriedly dresses, jumps into the car, and drives to the warehouse. Māris and Gunārs are standing at the gate, smoking, grinning.

—You get enough sleep, princess?

—That's captain to you! Kristofs growls into his beard, but doesn't take it to heart.

The men are joking. They truly are a great group. They work like horses and don't talk back much. And the princess jokes are just because he's young. Too young for this old-man-of-the-sea business. That's what they tell him. And maybe they're right, but Kristofs doesn't dwell on it.

There's a mist on the water. Kristofs fills his lungs with the damp air and smiles. He doesn't feel alone here. It may be the only place in the world where he feels at home.

While Kristofs maps out the day, the men chop fish for chum. Large knives, practiced movements, bundled up in their waterproof coveralls and hoods. The gulls don't approach, but, having smelled the fish, cry out pleadingly.

The chum goes in the traps, the traps go in the water, the pull, the drag, the catch—the men work like a single, wordless machine that can't function without all its parts.

Kristofs glances at his phone once they're far from shore. It's only then that he sees the message from his sister.

—Fuck!

—What's up? Māris yells.

—My sister. The baby's coming early. I don't know, her text doesn't make much sense, but I've got to go.

—Now? The men all give him a look.

—Mmhm, Kristofs grunts, adding, Yes, tonight.

—And what're we supposed to do? C'mon, man, this wasn't the plan, the men say. The open sea is no place for women and babies and men who drop it all when summoned.

—I'll get you guys placed, he says curtly and purses his lips.

A wrinkle forms across his brow and his eyes narrow. The men know this look, and they say nothing. If Kristofs says he'll find them work, he will. And he does. He spends all day looking, but he finds something. The men stop their grumbling.

Kristofs tries to focus, but Matilde keeps forcing her way into his thoughts.

—Still thinking about the baby? Gunārs comes over at some point and puts a hand on his shoulder.

—Yeah . . .

—It'll be alright, kid. Women always manage!

—Lūkass is staying with a neighbor. Someone I don't know.

—Ah . . . Gunārs says and scratches his head.

Kristofs is a little angry with his sister. Where do these kids come from? Does she make the rounds herself or do the men come to her? He has no idea who Lūkass's father is, and now there's another on the way. Like some kind of Virgin Mary, babies out of the blue. Chosen ones. And sure, Lūkass is special. Kristofs loves him more than anything in the world.

—You're spoiling him, Matilde always says.

—Then find someone to actually raise him! Kristofs had once snapped, and Matilde's large eyes suddenly grew wet.

She didn't reply, simply wrapped her arms around herself and walked away.

That was the only time he said anything. Even when he'd come home to find her with a swollen belly yet again, he said nothing. He sent her money, helped around the house, fixed the roof, mowed the grass.

—Fuck! he shouts again, and then his vision goes black as a rogue trap full of crabs and lobsters crashes into his stomach.

He gasps for air and searches for a light in his darkness, unsure how he's still standing with the wind and world knocked out of him. He's reeling, but upright.

Once he's able to breathe and see again, he pulls up his sweater. His entire stomach is scarlet, as if sunburnt.

—Hey, you okay? Māris asks, rattled.

—Yeah . . . Kristofs wheezes, still unable to speak.

Words hurt, breathing hurts. He tries to walk and it hurts. The men watch him warily. He gestures to the trap. They understand, and get back to work.

That night he throws some clothes in a bag and rushes to the airport. There are no more seats on the late flight. He'll have to wait till morning.

He spends the night at the airport. Tries to sleep, but can't. His stomach is in agony. Two women sit across from him, wrapped in threadbare shawls. Watching him with black eyes. Perhaps waiting for him to fall asleep, so they can sneak over to his bag and . . . steal? What, his boxers? Socks? Kristofs grins at the thought. They can present these spoils to their husbands, who will then proudly show them off to their warrior friends: Look, the socks of a great white giant!

The airport is dead quiet. Kristofs texts Matilde.

"Where's Lūkass?"

. . .

"Who's this neighbor?"

. . .

"How are you?"

. . .

"You okay?"

But Matilde doesn't answer because she's fighting. For the baby, for herself. For herself as Lūkass's mother, as Kristofs's sister.

Kristofs hears gulls. He looks up and furrows his brow. The airport is free of birds, they're not allowed in here. He's the one crying out, from deep inside himself.

CHAPTER 3

The strong late-spring sunlight fills the room, and Lūkass opens his eyes. Rute smiles at him, but the boy is scared.

—Want breakfast? She asks.

—Mamma? he asks in reply and glances around.

—Still at the doctor's, but she'll be home later, Rute says not knowing if it's okay to make that kind of promise.

Rute doesn't know what "later" means to a kid.

—Hungry? she asks again, and Lūkass crawls out from under the blanket.

They go to the kitchen together, and Rute crouches next to the stove.

—I'll light a fire. So it'll be warmer.

Lūkass looks around with curiosity. Then he runs to the table and climbs onto a stool. Rute's worried he'll fall, so she rushes over to put a hand behind him, but he pushes her away. Rute decides to trust him and goes back to the stove. She wants coffee, but since Jūle didn't have an electric kettle, she has to light a fire each time.

Lūkass reaches over the table and takes some bread. One slice, straight from the bag, and bites into it.

—Butter! the boy demands, and Rute brings him butter.

For a second she wonders whether he knows how to butter his own bread, but then decides: if she's going to be looking after him, better keep the knife out of reach. Rute butters a slice of bread for herself and one for Lūkass; then they eat.

Afterward he wants to explore the entire house. He opens cupboards and climbs onto every chair. Jumps on the bed. Rute doesn't let him go into the spare room.

—There's nothing there, she says, but in truth she doesn't let him because not even she knows what's in there.

—What's that? Lūkass asks about anything he doesn't recognize.

An old coffee grinder, with a hand crank. A gadget for winding yarn. A whetstone. A penholder. A kerosene lamp.

Suddenly Rute sees that the world is full of things she's unable to explain to a child. Things that are forgotten, unwanted. And then she says, simply:

—I don't know.

They call Matilde.

—I'm so glad you called! Matilde sounds tired, but happy. I'm, I mean, *we're* just fine. The baby's in an incubator, but the doctors say it'll be alright. I . . . she wants to say something, but her voice catches.

—How are you two? Lūkass, did you sleep? she asks, because Rute has put the phone on speaker so they can both talk to her.

—I miss Mamma! Lūkass replies.

—I miss you too, Lūkass, Matilde says, but I have to stay in the hospital a little bit longer. Lūkass! You have a brother! He's so small. Remember I told you how tiny he'd be?

—Like a bunny?

—Yes, almost! Matilde says, and a smile cracks Rute's face.

—Rute, thank you so much, Matilde begins, Kristofs will be home real soon, he'll come get Lūkass. He'll get there to-night, tomorrow morning at the latest. You'll be okay?

Rute wants to say that, no, she won't be okay, she doesn't know anything about kids, but she says nothing. She'll wait for Lūkass's father. Life happens when it happens, and she has to hold on.

—I will, Rute whispers.

She wants to ask what happened. If it was very painful, how she feels. But she doesn't. Matilde is still a stranger. Rute only met her yesterday.

—Lūkass, I love you, Matilde whispers before she hangs up.

Rute can sense Lūkass is about to cry again, so she says brightly:

—Should we go down to the river?

—I have to poop, Lūkass replies.

Rute has no clue what pooping means with a kid this small. All she has is the outhouse in the backyard. She takes Lūkass there and he pulls down his pants on his own and looks for where to sit. Rute coughs nervously and tries to carefully position him on the large seat. She's afraid he'll fall in, so she holds him. She's never been this close to someone while they're shitting, has never wiped another's ass. But now she's doing it. Lūkass isn't at all bothered, all of this is normal to him. Rute, however, is flustered.

Flustered, and wondering why she doesn't have children. Then she'd know how to wipe their bottoms and butter their bread.

—How old are you? she asks Lūkass.

—Three, the boy says and lifts three fingers.

—My sister was three when I was born. Just like you and your brother! Rute realizes, but Lūkass isn't listening.

Then they go down to the river. Lūkass wants a dried-up reed, and Rute goes down to the riverbank to break one off. Lūkass traces circles in the water with it, splashing in all directions. Then they go back inside. Rute adds more wood to the stove and makes tea. She finds some pencils and they color on old newspapers. Then they sit on the windowsill and watch the crows.

—Your dad'll be home soon, Rute says, and Lūkass looks thoughtfully at her.

—My dad?

—You know . . . Kristofs.

—Kristofs is Mamma's brother! Lūkass says with a proud smile. I like Kristofs! he adds with equal pride. When will he be here?

—I don't know, Rute hesitates. Your mom said maybe tonight, maybe tomorrow.

—When's tonight? Lūkass wants to know.

While she's explaining when tonight is, Lūkass crawls into the bed and under the blanket.

—Find me! he calls sleepily, but instead she hums until he drifts off.

When he wakes in the afternoon he's cranky. It's hard on Rute; she feels useless, doesn't know how to calm him down.

Lūkass whines, he wants his mom, wants Kristofs, but Kristofs doesn't arrive. Rute fries up some potatoes for the boy. She doesn't have any cream, and Lūkass starts to whine again. There are no children's books in the house, so Rute tells him her own stories. About a crow with a blue backpack that it fills with stones, about small children who rolled out a ball of dough so wide it covered the entire floor. Rute tells these stories, and Lūkass listens. He's different from Matilde. His hair is very pale, and his eyes aren't big like hers, but not small, either. *Probably like his father's*, Rute thinks.

That night they fall asleep side by side snuggled close in the small bed, with Lūkass holding tightly onto Rute's hand.

Dear Dina!

That was the first time a kid that little held my hand. He's three years old, and his baby brother was born today. Do you remember when you were three, and I was born?

Dina? When he touched my hand, I remembered your hand. How we used to be little with little hands. Do you remember, Dina, how happy those hands were?

CHAPTER 4

He arrives on the second day. Kristofs. Rute opens the door and balks. He's a giant compared to his sister. The cool morning air can't even slip past him into the room.

—Kristofs! Lūkass shouts and runs to him.

The boy jumps into Kristofs's arms and buries his face in his beard. Rute sees Kristofs wince in pain, but he stifles it and hugs Lūkass tightly. Rute wonders if she's ever seen such tenderness.

Then Kristofs looks to her.

—Hi! Thanks for looking after Lūkass.

—Mmhm, Rute grunts and waits.

—We'll be going now, Kristofs says and touches his nose to Lūkass's.

As they leave, they glance back and Kristofs adds:

—If you need anything . . .

Rute nods, but they don't see. The two figures walk off as she stands in the doorway, thinking. Matilde had said that the other day, too. Would they really help her if she asked? Would they rush over if she needed them?

The house feels empty without Lūkass. Rute hears a fly buzzing, hears the river through the window. She draws a deep breath and for the first time takes a good look around. Old floors. Old windows. Old stove and range. Old, old, old. It's the only word that comes to mind. Old shed and old flowerbeds, an old well, and the old willow in the yard.

The electricity had been cut when she'd first arrived several days ago. It had taken two days for her to figure out what the outstanding bill was so she could pay it, and another day before someone decided to get to work and turn the lights back on. The house has no central plumbing, just the outhouse around back. Drinking water comes from the well, and water for the dishes and laundry comes from the river. The water buckets themselves had been filthy; Rute spent a long time scrubbing them with sand from the river. She found a rake in the shed and cleaned up the yard. Old leaves and twigs. Old, everything old. Old crocuses in the flowerbed, old lily of the valley. Old, but blooming nonetheless! Rute wants to bloom like that, too. Let her stories, her past, lie with her, that's all fine. But she wants to bloom.

The house has two bedrooms, one of which Jūle had slept in, which is where Rute sleeps now. The second room is different entirely. There are a few blankets and a couple pillows laid out on the floor, a bookshelf along one wall filled with good but forgotten books. On the windowsill, a mug and an ashtray. Had people stayed in this room? Or maybe dogs? Was Jūle a smoker? Rute knows nothing about her father, doesn't even remember what he looks like. When they told her, "Your father has died," Rute had wanted to say, "Again?" Their whole lives she and her sister thought he was already dead. They never looked for him and didn't ask their mother much about him, either. When they did, she always told a different story. He'd been a good man, broad shouldered—or he'd been a weakling and the scum of the earth. Or a fool—their mother had said that once, too. The village idiot. The girls never asked again. Not Dina, not Rute.

But now Rute is here, in their father's home. She lies down on his bed and inspects her hands. The blisters on her fingers are healing; the skin is inflamed and stings. She's spent a lot of time with her hands in the cold river water, trying to scrub her father out of the house. So that she's the only one here.

Then Rute spends several days alone. No one comes looking for her. She reads Jūle's books and sits by the river. One day she finds an old bicycle in the shed and rides it to the only store around. She wanders the store and inspects the groceries for a long time, shopping with intent so she won't have to come back very often. The cashiers openly stare at her. Rute doesn't like that. She adds a tube of hand cream to her pile, pays, and leaves. Her backpack is heavy, and the old bike is tough to pedal. She should oil it, but she doesn't have the first clue how to do that. *Maybe ask Kristofs?* Rute thinks and pedals, her cheeks flushed. No, better not. Rute doesn't want people. People were what she had wanted to get away from. Why turn to them now?

She had walked away from people. From satin bedsheets, from a sink with hot and cold water, from a toilet that flushes. From an electric stove with a ceramic range, from a monthly appointment with her esthetician, from her hair stylist, from heated floors that allowed her to walk around barefoot all year. She'd even walked away from pedicures, yes, the polish now almost completely chipped off. There's no nail polish remover in Jūle's house, so Rute's toes are as they are. She does want to buy an electric kettle, though. Come summer she can't light the stove each time she wants coffee. She doesn't need a television, doesn't want to know what's happening back in the city. All she brought was her computer, so she can write letters to her sister.

As she rides up to the house, she sees people in the yard. Matilde, smiling and holding a tiny, swaddled bundle, comes to greet her, her large teeth gleaming.

—Rute! Lūkass calls. This is Niklāvs!

Kristofs stands behind them; Matilde herself looks like a child in comparison. They're all so tiny next to him. Rute suddenly feels she, too, is very small.

—Rute, we came to say thank you, Matilde smiles, and Kristofs hands her a large package wrapped in shiny paper.

Rute leans the bike against the shed and accepts the gift.

—Thank you! she says, but her voice is quiet and very far away.

Rute doesn't remember the last time she spoke. A week ago? She jumps at the sound of her own voice, how foreign it is.

—I saw you didn't have curtains in your room, Matilde says. I hope you'll like them. Jūle might not have needed them, but I think women need curtains. They make a place homier, no?

Rute doesn't know how to respond. Curtains? She wonders if she should tell them she's not planning on staying. She's only taking a break. At some point she'll have to go back to her life, because she does have one there, in the city. But now—curtains.

31

They all watch Rute and wait.

—Want help putting them up? Matilde asks, and it's only then Rute realizes she should invite them in.

They follow her into the house. Rute quickly lights the stove to boil water for coffee, and Lūkass shows his mother and Niklāvs all the strange objects in the kitchen. Rute unwraps the curtains. They're a sunny yellow and have that brand-new smell. Kristofs starts clipping rings onto them and Rute stands, embarrassed, not knowing what to say. No one has ever gifted her curtains. No man has ever clipped curtains onto a dusty curtain rod for her.

Then they drink coffee. Lūkass climbs into Rute's lap. Matilde extracts Niklāvs from the blanket, and it's the first time Rute has seen such a small baby this up-close. Niklāvs is very pale, with reddish fuzz on his head. If his hair were yellow, he'd look like a baby chick.

—Jūle's daughter? Kristofs asks suddenly, and Rute nods.

—I already told you! Matilde cuts in. There're two of you, right? she asks and stands.

She rocks Niklāvs in her arms and whispers something to him. Lūkass fidgets in Rute's lap; he wants sugar but Kristofs doesn't give him any.

—Yes, two of us, Rute finally replies.

—Is your sister coming? Matilde wants to know everything.

—No, Dina's not around.

—Oh, I get it. Kristofs lives far away, too, in England. He works on fishing boats. Tell her! Matilde encourages him, but Kristofs says nothing.

Rute doesn't ask, either, and Matilde doesn't force it.

—How old are you? Matilde says instead. She jumps freely from topic to topic. Even the way she rocks Niklāvs, the way she smiles with her big teeth, it's all so free.

—Thirty-six, Rute says and looks at Kristofs.

He's staring at her with surprise, like he's seeing her for the first time. Matilde laughs.

—Then you're the oldest here. I'm twenty-nine, Kristofs is twenty-seven.

—I'm three! Lūkass yells and raises three fingers.

The thought comes to Rute that Kristofs, Matilde, and the kids are the flowering crocuses out front, while she, Rute, is the old house. Matilde isn't laughing to be mean, but because she's surprised, as is Kristofs.

Rute is an old house. She thinks about this long after everyone has left. She doesn't have kids, doesn't want them, never has. She's never worked far away like Kristofs—has never really worked outside the home. She doesn't have thick, red hair, doesn't have a bright smile. An old, empty house coursing with the frigid blood of winter.

She goes to the mirror, braids her hair, and then wraps the braids into a pretzel. Her mother used to do her hair this way when she was little. Rute stares at herself for a long while. Even with a braid-pretzel on her head she's an old and empty house. When she goes down to the river for more water, she is shocked by her reflection. Then she laughs. She wants to hear if this old house can still laugh.

That night, Rute falls asleep staring at her sun-yellow curtains. She thinks of Kristofs. How does someone that young get to be that grown-up?

Sis!

Where do you work? Is it very far away? Why don't you ever answer? I'm sorry, I'm venting again. Sorry!

I have new curtains. Sun-yellow. I don't pull them closed at night. It's too lonely if I do. The apple trees, the moon, the river—it's fine if they can see inside. It's fine.

This house is built from cracks, the ones between old boards. And the only thing keeping the cracks together is the boards. The wind from the river fully fills a house like this. It's a strange feeling, like there's someone behind me, blowing their breath along the nape of my neck. And then I freeze and wait. I wait for lips to touch my skin, or a finger to trace a name along my shoulder. Or a sure hand to reach up and ruffle my hair. Like you do to those little gray dogs. But there's no one there. There never is. Just me and the river. Me in the river.

I love you, Dina!

CHAPTER 5

Well, finally! Rute stands by the old willow in the yard, watching it slowly come to life. The buds on its branches are growing plump, a few of them already split open. She'd been starting to think the old tree would never flower. That it would rot away and fall apart. She would've chopped it up and stacked the logs in the shed, and then stacked her faith in life along with them. But it's flowering. The sun is so bright and alive, and a laugh bubbles up inside her.

Then Kristofs walks into the yard. He's carrying a large melon and a plastic water bottle. Rute stands where she is and waits for him to approach.

—Hey! he says in his slightly hoarse voice.

—Hey! she replies.

Then he holds out the plastic bottle.

—Brought you some birch sap.

Rute takes the bottle.

—And a melon. He holds it out for her to take, but then stops and looks around for somewhere to put it.

—Come on in, she gestures to him to follow.

They go inside. Kristofs puts the melon on the kitchen table and stands, fidgeting.

—I wanted to ask you a favor, he begins, but doesn't continue.

—Oh?

—Can you make some coffee? I mean, that's not it, not what I—but . . . could you make some? Kristofs is still fidgeting.

Rute turns on her new electric kettle and slides a mug, the coffee, and the sugar over to him. She picks up a large knife and starts cutting the melon. She slices off the rind, removes the soft fruit, and cuts it into pieces. She wonders what else she can offer Kristofs to eat, but she doesn't have anything. Only yesterday's nettle soup, still in the pot. But she'd be embarrassed to offer him that. To her mind, men aren't the nettle-eating type.

She eats fairly simply: oatmeal, fried potatoes, macaroni boiled with milk. Yesterday she'd decided to cook nettle soup, the kind their mother used to make. It was good, edible. A long time ago she'd read that tree buds were good for you, so she'd even tried those but they weren't for her. She still eats a few every day despite not liking the taste. She could go to the store more often, but she doesn't want to.

—Want to eat outside? It's nice in the sun, Kristofs suggests, and she nods.

They sit on an old wooden bench under the kitchen window. Rute holds the plate of melon on her lap. She takes a piece and carefully puts it in her mouth. Juice trickles down her chin and oh!, when's the last time she ate something like this?

—I have a favor to ask, Kristofs says again. I leave in a couple days and . . . well . . . Matilde is by herself, with the kids. Can you look out for her? he says, staring into the distance.

Rute almost chokes on the melon, and it's just as well. No answer needed. She coughs, and Kristofs thumps her on the back. They drink their coffee in silence.

—Yours? Kristofs stands and walks over to where her bike is propped up against the shed.

—Got a screwdriver? He doesn't wait for a reply. Instead, he goes into the shed and comes out with a screwdriver, a hex-key, and a small oilcan. He flips the bike upside-down and works in silence. Tightening, adjusting. Oils the chain and the gears. Rute watches him and slowly eats more melon.

—Jūle didn't bike.

She winces at the mention of her father.

—He was a walker. Walked everywhere all the time. He was, well, a little different. Know why?

No, she doesn't. She never knew her father.

—He helped a lot of people. *A lot* a lot. I don't know anyone else who would do what he did.

Rute says nothing, and Kristofs continues:

—He'd bring home old groceries from the store. They weren't bad, just past their expiration date. He'd cook huge pots of food and bring it to those in need. Old people with little to no pension. Single mothers and their kids . . . We'd help drive him around sometimes. The store knew Jūle would come for the expired stuff, and they'd set it aside for him.

Now Rute understands the large pots in the kitchen. She'd thought they'd been for dog food . . .

—And the blankets on the floor? she asks, though she still feels like she doesn't want to know.

—Oh, that's for people who had nowhere else to go. Jūle never turned anyone away, see? Not even the biggest drunk. Could you do that for a guy whose wife just kicked him out of the house? Or for someone just out of prison? Like this one guy . . . Kristofs shakes his head slowly, I don't know—I've thought about it a lot, but there's no way I could, not me, no chance.

He stands to flip the bicycle back upright, then props it against the shed and turns to Rute.

—Jūle could see the person inside them, y'know?

She flushes from the directness of his stare. She looks down at the plate and scratches its edge with a fingernail. Kristofs comes over and drains the last of his coffee.

—If you need anything from the store, or a ride somewhere, just ask Matilde. I'll leave my car with her. Maybe the two of you want to go into the city some day?

—No! Rute blurts, and then repeats more calmly: Not me, thanks, I don't want to.

Kristofs raises his eyebrows, but she doesn't elaborate.

—I'll look after her! Rute calls after him, and she imagines he's smiling.

And he is, but she can only see his large, broad back moving away.

Dear Dina!

I have a feeling our dad was no village idiot, unlike what Mom always said. But if he was, he was a kind one. Kristofs said that Jūle could see the person inside everyone.

I'm supposed to look after Matilde, Kristofs's sister. She has two sons, Lūkass and Niklāvs. I have no idea what it means to look after someone. Am I supposed to go visit her now and again? Is that enough? Talk with her? Babysit? I don't know that I can even do that.

Dina, are there buds on the trees where you are? Do you eat them? I don't like them. I keep trying, but still can't get into them.

Sis, if you knew how much I miss you! It's been almost ten years since I last saw you. Hah! I don't know about you, but on the tenth anniversary, I'm going to howl. I'll go down to the river, fall to my knees, and howl. One of these days you'll have to hear me, and then you'll have to howl back.

Dina, you're my anger, my desire, my pain. You are such a strong part of me, such an empty part . . . Dina, am I your empty part, too? Can you live with that emptiness?

I can't. Not anymore.

But the neighbors bring me curtains and oil my bike, and I bought an electric kettle and laugh about the flowering buds on the willow tree.

Yesterday I thought the river might be in pain. That it carries too much.

This emptiness is so goddamn empty.
Love you.

CHAPTER 6

The trees are green with leaves when Kristofs comes back. He goes down to the river and stares at it for some time. The river is a road to the sea. His sea, with its crabs and traps, its storms and lulls, where grinning dolphins sometimes dance around the boats. Where he doesn't feel alone.

You're never alone with seagulls, an old gull had once said to him, crying the words into his flesh.

Lūkass is like a burr, at his side all night. Matilde is happy as well and starts dinner. Niklāvs has grown, his body made of little rolls of fat. Kristofs is afraid to pick him up; he doesn't know his own strength sometimes, his hands hard and strong from the sea. Numb to tenderness. Sometimes he accidentally squeezes Lūkass too hard and then the boy cries. Lūkass is a big kid, though. Niklāvs is so small, fragile.

In the morning Kristofs wakes to the sound of Matilde talking to someone in the kitchen. Rute? The voice is familiar, and it occurs to Kristofs that he hasn't heard Rute talk very much. He might not even remember what her voice sounds like.

He goes into the kitchen. It is Rute, sitting with Matilde at the table, both talking in low voices. Rute looks different—her hair is down, which makes her face look softer. She looks very pretty this morning. The sun shines across her face.

—Morning! he says softly, and Rute smiles.

It's the first time he's seen her smile. It's a nice smile. It brings millions of little lines to the corners of her eyes.

—Good morning! both women reply.

—Shh! The boys are still asleep! Matilde puts a finger to her lips.

Kristofs nods and heads to the bathroom. He showers and thinks about Rute, there in the kitchen. About how her smile seemed to say: "See, I looked after Matilde!"

He hears the boys wake up, and then they all eat breakfast together. Lūkass, of course, sits in his lap. Rute doesn't talk much, but smiles often.

—We should plant the potatoes, Matilde says. I already reserved a tractor.

—To dig furrows, she explains; she thinks Rute doesn't know anything about planting potatoes.

But Rute knows. She planted many, many potatoes as a child. In fields large and small. Fields with rocky soil, and fields with soil as black as the darkest thoughts.

—Tomorrow? Kristofs suggests, but Matilde shakes her head.

—Niklāvs has a doctor's appointment tomorrow.

—Rute and I can do it, right? Kristofs looks at Rute, and she nods in agreement. Someone would have to watch the boys anyway, he adds.

—I'll plant potatoes too! Lūkass shouts and goes to find his shovel and pail. Mamma, I want potatoes! Are you going to fry some?

Matilde laughs and explains that you don't eat the old potatoes. They don't taste good.

—Yes they do! They do! Lūkass insists.

Then Matilde picks up Niklāvs and goes to the bedroom, where she lies down to nurse him.

Kristofs, Lūkass, and Rute stay in the kitchen.

—How were things here? Kristofs asks.

Lūkass runs to get his new book from England. He wants to show it to Rute.

—Good, Rute replies, and then after a pause asks: And you?

Kristofs smiles. He remembers the crabs and the lobsters, remembers the sound of the sea buffeting the coast. Would Rute understand? Can he talk to her about the gulls? About freedom?

—Like every spring. The crabs practically fall into the traps, hungry and a little dazed—and our crew is happy.

Then he scratches his head, his fingers disappearing into his thick, coarse hair. It's stronger than Rute's hair, hair ravaged by the sea winds and soaked by salt water.

—It was exhausting, he admits. Spring takes a lot of hard work.

Then Lūkass runs back into the kitchen and shows Rute the book from England. In it is a story about a little girl who has a baby brother.

—Just like me! Lūkass says, and Rute smiles at him.

Kristofs watches and thinks they should plant extra potatoes for her. Their field is big, there'll be enough for everyone.

Rute is back at their house the next morning. The furrows have already been dug, and Kristofs has brought the bags of potatoes to the edge of the field.

—Matilde left you a pair of boots. Will they fit? he hands Rute the rubber boots and she removes the orange wool socks stuffed inside.

—They'll fit.

Matilde is a lot shorter than Rute, but they have the same shoe size. Good thing. Rute only brought the one pair of shoes. If she wore her shoes in the potato field, she'd have to wash them. And what would she wear while they were drying?

The field isn't huge, but it takes them more time than anticipated. Kristofs heads to the farthest ends of the furrows, Rute stays at this end. There's not a lot of opportunity to talk, but neither of them is much of a talker. Rute walks and drops potatoes into the furrows with practiced movements. Take a step, drop a potato; if it starts to roll away stop it with your foot. It's like riding a bike, or swimming: you learn how to do it once and you remember it for life.

The basket is heavy; after a while it starts to strain her arm. Rute switches sides, but it's harder to work left-handed. She secretly observes Kristofs. He's carrying his bag as if it were a paper sack of feathers. If you blew on it they'd float away. A sea-giant in the middle of a potato field. A laugh bursts from her and Kristofs looks up from his end of the furrows. He gives her a questioning toss of his head, but she waves him off.

When they've finished, Kristofs fills both baskets with the leftover seedling potatoes.

—You have any at home? he asks Rute.

—A few. I got some at the store, she answers.

—I'll bring these over, he says and heads in the direction of her house.

Rute hurries to grab her shoes. She'll return Matilde's boots later, once she's cleaned them and washed the socks.

—Shed? Kristofs asks, and Rute nods.

He puts the baskets away, but doesn't leave. He wants to stay with her a while longer. Rute goes into the house, and he follows. She fills a bowl with water and after she washes her hands she pours clean water for Kristofs. He scrubs his hands with a towel and can feel Rute's hands in it, even though she's crouching next to the stove. Rute breaks up kindling, her thoughts thick. Why doesn't he go home? What does he want?

—I'll stay and eat with you, Kristofs says, and she nods again.

There's not much to eat in the house. Without a word, she starts to peel potatoes to fry up with sausages. Kristofs has gone into the spare room and is standing at the bookshelf, leafing through a book.

—He'd read to them, he suddenly says.

—Who? Rute asks from the kitchen.

—Jūle. He'd say: if you want to stay here, you'll have to listen. And they listened. Even the totally, completely drunk ones. Somehow they heard him.

Rute is silent. She doesn't know how to talk about Jūle, this man who was her father. She doesn't want to. She frowns and scrapes the potatoes to one side of the pan before adding pieces of sausage.

When the food is ready, Rute serves it and they sit down at the kitchen table. Kristofs takes up a fork in his giant hand and starts to eat—although Rute would call it inhaling. Bite after bite goes into his mouth, faster and faster. He spears a piece of sausage and shoves it in.

But then Rute places a hand on his hand. The fork stops, and Kristofs looks up in surprise. She carefully takes the fork from him, spears some potatoes, and slowly brings the fork to his mouth. Flustered, he glances from the fork to her, but opens his mouth. She slowly feeds him the potatoes and then some sausage, just as slowly. Some oil from the sausage drips onto his beard and he lets her wipe it off. Slowly. Rute doesn't know what she wants for herself but she suddenly wants this giant to slow down. The fork in her hand moves slowly, Kristofs's mouth moves slowly. Rute feeds him, fills him with her act of feeding him. She feeds him slower than you'd feed a child, draws the moment out more and more. When the food is gone, she clears the dishes and puts them in the large washing bowl. Then, wordlessly, she takes the bowl and sits down on a small stool by the stove.

Kristofs stands and goes to the door. He turns, ready to say something.

—Rute . . . he begins, but stops. Then he leaves.

He leaves and he thinks. Thinks about his grandma, about hunger, about the dried-out bread crusts the neighbors would bring over for their chickens, but that he and Matilde would keep and happily gnaw on. He remembers the cake box a bakery driver once brought them. A huge box, filled with smashed eclairs and shortbread, Napoleon and Vecrīga cakes. Some of the cream in the pastries had gone sour, even started to mold, but he and Matilde had eaten all of it. Their hunger drove them on, faster and faster. And that's stayed with him. He doesn't know how to eat slow anymore. But then here comes Rute and wants things to be different. Shit! He's angry he let her do that. He's so angry that he snaps at Lūkass and ignores Matilde completely. He disappears into the bathroom, takes off his dirty clothes, and steps into the shower. *A waterfall*, he thinks, and closes his eyes.

CHAPTER 7

Rute wakes with potato soil in every pore. Such a sensation of filth that she grabs a towel and goes to the river. The water is cold, but Rute wants to feel alive and clean. It's her first time going in. She swims quickly to the opposite bank—the river isn't wide. On the swim back, she stops in the middle for a bit and feels for the current, gets to know it. It doesn't sweep her away, but it also doesn't let her remain in place. It takes strength to remain within yourself. She scrambles out. It's cold and she's smiling from ear to ear with the feeling that she's toppled a mountain, that she could topple a hundred more. She heads up to the house and sees Matilde standing at the door.

—Hey! Rute calls to her.

The unexpected "hey" from behind makes Matilde jump and she whips around, but when she sees Rute she smiles.

—Go for a swim? she asks when she sees the towel in Rute's hands and her damp hair.

—I did! First time this year!

—You're crazy . . . You know it's only May, right?

—I know, it was cold, Rute laughs.

Matilde is holding a sizeable bag, which she gives to Rute.

—For you, she says. I was at the thrift store and got you some things. I hope they'll fit.

And since Rute stands staring, silent, Matilde adds:

—Oh stop, I know you don't have a lot of clothes. You need more. You can't wear the same shirt every day and hope to god it always dries on time.

—Thanks, Rute murmurs and brings the bag inside.

Then they drink coffee. Rute butters a slice of bread for herself; she hasn't eaten breakfast.

—Kristofs is watching the kids, thank god! Matilde is chatty. It's exhausting being with them all the time. Don't get me wrong, I love them more than anything, but sometimes you need to get away, y'know?

Rute is very familiar with the need to get away. She sometimes wants to get away from herself, but that's harder to do.

—Want to go into the city while he's here? We could grab a beer, go dancing.

—No! Rute says curtly.

Matilde's eyes widen, but she doesn't ask. After a moment, she laughs.

—Can you imagine? I don't know how to swim! Even though I live right by the river.

—Are you afraid to? Rute asks.

—No, not afraid, although . . . maybe I am. When I was really little our grandma drowned some kittens. Put them all in a bag and tied it shut, then carried it to the river. Shoved the bag underwater and held it there for a long time. Afterward she buried the bag under an apple tree. I followed her and saw everything. Heard it. Those kittens, mewling the entire time. Even when the bag went into the water. Our grandma, she sobbed through all of it. Kept crying after, too. That's why that river . . . I can't.

She takes a sip of coffee and looks out the window.

—Did you live with your grandma full time? Rute asks.

—Are you asking if we're orphans? Matilde laughs again, but Rute no longer understands her laughter. No, we have parents. Both mom and dad. You'll probably meet them someday, they come down once a year. Although sometimes not that often.

Rute is sorry she asked. Matilde's expressions are screaming that it's all much more painful than she lets herself believe.

—We were a burden to them. Me and Kristofs, when we were little. They'd even bought these special harnesses for us, for when we went out. So we wouldn't run around, touch everything, do whatever kids do. So they could control our so-called bad behavior. Grandma always said that's what kids do, but our parents didn't want kids like that. And when they decided to send us both to a kind of reform school, Grandma took us in instead. Our parents didn't even object. They'd come visit sometimes, but less and less. I think everyone in the city eventually forgot they even had kids.

And then Matilde's smile is gone and she starts to cry.

—I haven't talked about it in so long . . . she apologizes, and Rute gives her a moment.

—You don't have to. I'm sorry I asked, I honestly didn't know . . . Rute murmurs; she knows that prying into someone else's life never ends well.

—Hey, it's fine. It's okay. Y'know, it was at Grandma's that we finally started to come alive. She taught us so many things our parents never did. How to cut with a knife, how to hammer nails, wash dishes, pick out bread at the store. Grandma was pretty poor, we were hungry a lot, but hunger is a hundred times better than parents like ours. It really is, and here Matilde smiles again, sadly.

—I still remember how it felt, the tug of the . . . the harness when they wanted us to stop. Like a puppet on a string . . . Kristofs doesn't remember, he was too young. Thank god.

Rute thinks about children on leashes. How do they live, or survive? Her childhood was the opposite. She and her sister had been so little when they'd been pushed—again and again—out of the nest. Soon as they managed to climb back in—another push. They had to learn to take care of themselves at an extremely young age. It occurs to Rute that that was better than being tied to a leash. She never wants to be tied down. Never.

—Oh hey! I brought you something else! Matilde says and they go out to the yard.

There's another bag next to the fence. Matilde takes out some dahlia bulbs.

—Dahlias? Rute is surprised.

—I found them in the cellar. I brought them up and figured I had too many. I'm not going to plant all of them. So I brought some for you, Matilde says cheerfully.

—I don't know . . . Rute sighs.

—Yes, you do. Grab a shovel and dig! Not too deep, though, the soil is clayey, she adds, and then she's off toward the gate.

Rute manages to catch a "the kids probably miss me" and a "see you!" And then she is alone with her dahlia bulbs.

Dear sis!

I planted the dahlias. For you. I dug up the ground with a dull shovel and tore out the weeds. Matilde was right—the soil here is all clay. But I planted the bulbs and did some thinking. Ten years. Do you still remember me? Or think of me? Are you planting dahlias for me, somewhere?

Life seems to happen on its own. I would've never guessed that I'd one day be planting dahlias at our dad's house. Never. But life happens. In all kinds of ways.

Sis, I want to tell you about the river. About me in the river. It makes me tremble and shiver. It makes me laugh. It's been so long since I've felt this alive. The water is fairly clear by the dock. Deep. I can't touch the bottom, I'd have to go under a bit. You can cross it in no time. If you want get a good swim in you have to kind of circle around. You can feel the current. If you let it, it'll carry you, though I don't know how far.

Sis! I want to stay in the river.

I wish you'd come back . . .

Love you.

CHAPTER 8

It's been raining for several days and Kristofs is thinking about the sea. And yes, also about Rute, the strange woman next door. He wants to see her again before he leaves. Just to be near her. But he can't think of a reason to go over. Once, when he and Matilde were heading into the city with the kids, he'd suggested taking Rute with them.

—No, she won't come. She doesn't want to go to the city, Matilde had said, and Kristofs hadn't pressed the issue.

—If she doesn't, she doesn't. But why? People can't live without cities. How long can Rute hold out?

The day before he leaves, Kristofs asks Lūkass:

—Want to go see Rute?

—Yes, yes! Lūkass is delighted, and when a surprised Rute opens the door Kristofs says:

—Lūkass wanted to see you!

—Ah, okay. Come on! Rute steps back to let them into the kitchen.

—Coffee? she asks.

Lūkass declines, but Kristofs nods. Rute cuts a slice of rye bread for Lūkass, and the boy holds it hungrily in both hands. They sit around the kitchen table in silence. Lūkass holds the bread a little too tightly and it starts to crumble, falling onto the floor. He slides off the stool and picks up the pieces with his little fingers. Rute thinks you could keep chickens in the house with a kid like him, always leaving behind a trail of crumbs. The chickens would be content, and so would the kid's mother.

—Will you turn on the radio? she asks Lūkass, and the boy nods happily.

He pushes a stool over to the windowsill where the radio sits, and turns the knob. Then he dances for a second before running into the bedroom. He has to see everything, inspect everything. And Rute's house has so much to see! Books and all kinds of things. Lūkass likes the coffee grinder best. Kristofs and Rute hear the boy singing a folk song:

"*Tūdaliņ, tāgadiņ, man tā kurpe pušums . . .*"

—*Pušu!* Kristofs corrects, calling to the other room.

The little voice stops for a second, and then starts again:

"*Tūdaliņ, tāgadiņ, man tā kurpe pušums . . .*"

Kristofs raises his palms in defeat.

—I'm going home tomorrow.

—Home? Rute looks up.

—Back to sea, I mean. To England, he explains.

—You call the sea home?!

—Don't know. I guess. That's what it feels like.

Rute glances out the window.

—The river is home, too. For me. That's how I feel.

53

—The river is a road to the sea, Kristofs adds.

Then Lūkass bursts in.

—Why do skeletons live in graves? he asks Kristofs.

—I don't know. Why?

—Because they're hiding, he answers and dashes out again.

Rute wonders how so much energy can fit into one child. Had she and Dina been that energetic too? Or Kristofs and Matilde, on their leashes? She glances at Kristofs and tries to imagine him on a leash. Could you even tie up something that big? Kristofs is giant, he'd only have to breathe in and a harness like that would snap in half.

Then this giant man lifts a hand and touches a finger to a scar on her arm. It's a small mark, from some vaccine or other, Rute doesn't remember what kind. She's never thought about it. But now Kristofs is holding one strong hand right above it, touching it ever so lightly. She takes a deep breath and pulls away. Then she stares deep into his eyes.

—You're cold. I'll light the stove, he says and stands.

—It's fine, there's not a lot of firewood left, Rute says, but then reconsiders. Alright, go ahead.

Kristofs takes the firewood basket and goes to the shed. He sees the flowerbed in the garden and sees that the old bushes have been trimmed. The shirt Rute had been wearing when he first met her is hung out to dry. He fills the basket with firewood and brings it back to the house. Rute and Lūkass are in the bedroom, laughing about something. Kristofs lights the stove and goes to them. They've crawled under the blanket on the bed and Lūkass is playing with a flashlight.

—Oooo, I'm going to eat you! Rute is saying.

—We're playing with shadows, she tells Kristofs, emerging from under the blanket, hair tousled.

Kristofs smiles.

—I'll write to you, sometime. From out at sea, okay? he asks, and Rute freezes.

Her face hardens and her jaw clenches.

—Don't worry about it, Rute says.

—Okay. Then you write me, Kristofs jokes, even though Rute's words hurt more than a crab trap to the stomach.

It's time for them to go. Kristofs remembers Matilde telling them not to stay long. Rute gives Lūkass a squeeze and wishes Kristofs calm waters. Kristofs gives no reply; he lifts Lūkass onto his broad shoulders and they leave.

Rute goes down to the river and sits for a while. The riverbank is damp. The air smells of sweet flag and seaweed, of smoke and wet moss. A bit like autumn, even though it's summer. She sheds her clothing and slides into the water. She lets it carry her as she floats on her back and stares at the sky. Now and then she moves her arms and legs to stay floating in the middle of the river, where there is a lot of seaweed. Once there she finds a spot where the current can't carry her any farther, and she floats in place, feeling the seaweed swirl and wrap around her like so many snakes. Rute speaks the river's words in her mind, though she has no idea where they come from. She speaks and speaks and speaks, and then suddenly a rough hand grabs her and yanks her ashore. It's Kristofs. He's glaring bug-eyed at her, terrified, like he's about to scream, but then he lets go and she drops to the ground. She is tangled and wrapped up, so full of the river's words that her legs fail her. Kristofs takes off his shirt and thrusts it at her. Only then does she remember she is completely naked. Kristofs turns and slowly trudges up the path, the one cleared by fishermen, and goes home. She follows. They don't speak, simply walk.

—Did you know that caravan camels get left along the side of the trails to die? They work and work, carrying things until they lose all strength, and then they're just abandoned. Even if they've been with the caravan for years and years. Even then.

Rute talks, but Kristofs's back remains silent. He shows no sign of having heard her. Just keeps walking, one long stride after another.

—The trails are like camel cemeteries, she continues. And the vultures circle above them . . . Sometimes they don't even wait until . . . How can you just abandon someone who's been by your side and carried you for so long? Just leave them behind?

Kristofs's back is still silent. He passes the old dock and disappears into the reeds and cattails.

That night, Rute has a dream. She needs to move forward, but can't. She stands in the middle of a road, but the road ahead is covered in snakes. Big, fat ones. They slither and slither like the seaweed in the river. Black with glossy, yellow heads. Rute stands all alone and can't get anywhere. Then someone scares off the snakes, and she wakes up drenched in sweat. Kristofs?

CHAPTER 9

Dina!

This is such a strange summer. Warm and full of berries. I spend a lot of time in the river; my hair barely has time to dry before I'm sinking back in. The river is where my fish live, the bottom scattered with chunks of clay. The river is the older sister to my despair. I think about that a lot. About how vast that kind of despair can be. Do you remember how desperate Aigars was when he didn't have money for cigarettes? Remember how he took a crowbar to the floorboards, pried them up because . . . maybe an old butt had fallen between the cracks. And he found one. Snatched it up, brushed off the dust, and brought it to his lips with a trembling hand. That's how vast despair can get. So vast that you're ready to rip everything up, tear it to shreds, and break it. Break yourself into shards and then pick yourself back up with trembling hands.

The river is the older sister to that kind of despair. It takes you in and cradles you. Lulls you back to life.
Dina, what am I going to do when summer is over?
Sending hugs.

One morning Rute goes for a walk under the apple trees. She picks up a large, juicy apple and bites into it, letting the juice linger on her lips. The grass is still dewy, her feet are freezing. Suddenly, a small car pulls into the driveway with a trailer filled with firewood. A man she doesn't know hops out of the car and approaches her.

—Morning, ma'am! Brought your firewood, he says and gestures to the trailer. Where d'you want it?

Rute's eyes dart around, unsure, and she finally points to the shed.

—I didn't order wood, she says, but the man keeps working.

—All I know is I was told to bring it to Jūle's place, he says with a laugh.

Rute throws the half-eaten apple aside and goes to help the man. They both toss firewood down from the trailer; the yard smells of pitch. Once the trailer is empty, the man sits on the bench in front of the house. Takes a crumpled pack out of his pocket and lights a cigarette. He has a very suntanned face and hair that's going gray.

—This is a good house, ma'am. A good man lived here, he says.

—I never knew him, she replies.

—You're Jūle's daughter?

—Yes.

—Then you knew him. He'll always be part of you.

In that moment she wants to know more about her father.

—How did you know him?

—I came here a few times. When things were real bad. Jūle was the only one who didn't turn me away, the man smiles. Nights he'd sit on a little stool and read to me. Think it was Tolstoy. *War and Peace*. I'd never read a book my whole life.

—Why did the others turn you away?

The man is silent for a minute. Then he scratches the back of his head and says:

—Used to hit my wife. One time I hit her too hard.

—That's horrible. Hard for me to hear that. Hard for any woman to hear that, Rute says, and the man lowers his head, but then he jerks it back up.

—You have his eyes. And his voice.

The man gets up and offers her his hand. She shakes it, but then says:

—Wait!

She runs into the bedroom and finds Tolstoy's *War and Peace*.

—This is for you! From Jūle, she adds, and the man squeezes his eyes shut.

When his moment of wanting to cry passes, the man takes the book in his calloused hands and gets in his car.

Dear Dina!

I went to the cemetery today. It's a nice, small cemetery, filled with good. I don't know why people avoid cemeteries. I don't know why they're afraid of them. Cemeteries are full of life, too. Good life. You don't go to a cemetery with bad thoughts. With sad ones, yes, of course, but not with bad ones.

I brought Dad an apple. The bumper crop has ripened. I couldn't find his grave at first and asked some elderly woman. Turns out Dad's buried right next to his parents. Our grandparents. Gran and Gramps.

Then I started to really miss all of you. You, Dad, Gramps and Gran—who I didn't even know about. You're all there, somewhere.

I don't want you all to leave me alone anymore.

Love you.

That night Rute stacks the firewood in the shed. She stacks all of it, then sits down to rest her tired arms. It's already late, but she still wants to clean up. She heads down to the river. Swims and thinks about Kristofs. Suddenly the river turns salty, like Kristofs's sea. She feels its saltiness on her cheeks and a humid sea breeze. She whispers into the river, "Thank you for the firewood." The river is a road to the sea. Maybe he'll hear her.

Sis!

I turned my phone on for the first time in all these months. I needed to take a photo of the river. To stop it. Immortalize it.

You'd like it here. All the flowers, the books. A nesting crow, a crow with its chicks, flight. The fish in the river.

The buttercups. The river is intention and continuation. Something that never stops.

You'd like it here.

Lūkass. He's an amazing kid! One day he asked me: Why are giraffes yellow? I said I didn't know, and then he answered his own question: Because giraffes like the color yellow. He can't pronounce Ls yet. Giraffe sounds like gilaff. So: Gilaffs like the color yellow. His world has an answer for everything.

Niklāvs is still tiny. He and Matilde are like one person. Both with red hair and huge eyes. Matilde never really complains about her life. She is full of joy and the will to live. Once she wanted to tell me why the boys don't have a father. But instead she just said: "I really want to live. Just live . . ." And I totally get it. She doesn't ask anything of anyone, doesn't judge, doesn't expect. Just lives. Laughs loudly with those big teeth. Brought me a flower crown for Midsummer day. She gives tarot readings and only sees the good in the cards. Supposedly I'm going to enjoy a beautiful old age. Be surrounded by people. And lots of love.

I asked if my sister was one of those people. Matilde just laughed, said the cards don't say who the people are. Like I said—she only sees the good in them.

Sis! Dear, dear sis . . .

Rute can feel it has to be today. She packs her clothes in her backpack, unplugs the electric kettle, and makes sure all the lights are turned off. Locks the front door and picks all the dahlias. Then she goes to see Matilde.

Matilde opens the door and looks at Rute in wonder.

—I'm going, Rute says and swallows the lump in her throat.

—What do you mean, going? Matilde doesn't understand.

—I have to go back, I'm almost out of money . . . Rute explains awkwardly.

—Where are you going?

—Home.

—Home? Isn't this home?

—No, it's not. I don't know. Rute truly doesn't know the answer or what to say.

—Ruteeeee! Lūkass runs happily out of the room and throws his arms around Rute's legs.

She caresses his head.

—Rute, Rute! Come in! Come see what I made! Lūkass says impatiently.

—Not now, Lūkass, Rute's going.

—Where? the boy's blue eyes search Rute's.

Rute crouches beside him.

—I live in the city. I was just here for the summer.

—When are you coming back? Lūkass only cares about when he'll see her again.

Rute raises her eyes to Matilde's. They tell her to lie.

—Very soon. I'll be back very soon.

Then Rute hands the bouquet of dahlias to Matilde.

—Thanks, Matilde whispers.

In the other room, Niklāvs starts to cry, and Matilde takes a deep breath.

—Can I be a little mad at you now? she asks.

—Of course, Rute nods.

Matilde hugs Rute tightly and whispers in her ear: "We'll be waiting." Then she and Lūkass head back inside.

Rute walks the dusty road into town. The bus leaves at eleven, but she has a long trip ahead of her.

Dina!

Everything inside me is screaming. I didn't even go down for one last look at the river. I couldn't do it.

Love you.

CHAPTER 10

The city isn't waiting for Rute, doesn't even notice her return. Everything is just as rushed as before. She walks slowly toward home and is a little afraid of running into someone she knows. What would she say if they asked?

She doesn't see Stefans's car out front. She walks up the stairs and unlocks the door to their apartment. Her heart is pounding, and the sound echoes against the white walls. It occurs to Rute that here, in the apartment, there are more rooms than at the river house. You could get lost in here. She takes off her dirty shoes and brings them to the garbage can in the kitchen. There, she takes off her socks, pants—everything, she takes off everything and stuffs it into the garbage. Takes the full bag out of the can and ties the ends in a knot. Then heads to the bathroom, glancing into the bedroom along the way. There are boxes stacked against the walls. Stefans has packed up her things. In the bathroom, her feet sink into the warm bath mat. Heated floors. The soles of her feet recoil at the forgotten warmth. She turns on the tap and sits on the edge of the tub, watching it slowly fill with water, and then lowers herself in. She goes completely under, eyes closed, and longs for the river. But the tub isn't the river. Isn't the older sister of her despair.

Rute soaks for a long while, trying to scrub the summer off herself. She wants to return to her former life. She has to return—this is what she tells herself. Because people live in cities, people go to work, and people don't up and leave their husbands or wives.

When night falls, Rute sits with a bit mug of tea on the large windowsill and looks out onto the city. She was born here, she always comes back. Her gray hair falling around her face, she wonders what to do with her life. Will the city take her back? Will the river house miss her?

She hears keys in the lock. Hears Stefans take off his shoes, hears him pause when he spots her backpack in the hall. Then he comes into the room. Sees her and stops in the doorway.

—Rute, he says and stands there.

He doesn't come closer. She can see he has a new wrinkle in his forehead. She sees exhaustion in his eyes and a few gray hairs. He's handsome, this Stefans of hers.

Then he goes to the boxes and slowly starts to unpack them. Puts her books back on the shelves, along with the little porcelain elephants she thought would bring her happiness. Then he breaks down. Falls to his knees on the ground and sobs, his hands pressed to his face. Rute hops off the windowsill and runs to him. Hugs him and rocks him. Sings the song she once sang for Lūkass, sings until Stefans has cried out everything he had been holding onto.

—You smell different, he says eventually.

You smell like home, she wants to reply, but doesn't.

Instead, she slowly lifts his shirt. Leans closer and inhales him. Bites his earlobe. Lets out a low growl. Wraps herself around him like seaweed. Stefans isn't gentle, and neither is she. Rute knows many types of hunger, and right now they are both starving. She fumbles for something to hold onto, she feels a bit dizzy, but the floor is so smooth, and they've already come this far. Stefans puts a hand on her hip and holds her tight. The only thing Rute wants is his skin. To crawl under it. Live with it. And then they both start to move. Tremble. The movement hurts a little, but all good things come with a bit of pain. All the things you can't live without. Rute slides her hand between her legs, and then moves Stefans's hand there. She thinks: Good thing the floor is warm.

Later that night she opens her eyes to find Stefans is awake. He's lying next to her, staring at the ceiling.

—Are you going to leave again? his voice is quiet.

—I don't know, she replies, truthfully.

—It's hard, Stefans says after a few moments, but she doesn't respond. She moves next to him and rests her hand over his heart.

In the morning they have breakfast and Stefans asks what she's going to do.

—Look for work, she says.

—You know you don't have to. I can give you money.

—No, I want to work.

And she adds:

—I need to work.

—Okay, I'll let my office know that you're back. Maybe they'll have something to send you, Stefans says, and Rute nods.

—I'll reach out to my people, too.

When Stefans heads out, Rute thinks about doing things. About planting potatoes, about dahlias, washing clothes in the cold river water. She thinks about playing with Lūkass and rocking Niklāvs in her arms. Then she goes to her room and turns on her computer. Opens a new page and stares at it. Rute likes her work—she likes translating, likes words and sentences. Likes to organize and reorganize them. Yes, she likes to reorganize. To seek out and change. She gets up and brings back the little elephants. The ones she had hoped would bring her happiness. Lines them up on the windowsill and gives each one a flick on the forehead.

And then she writes a letter to her mother. Just a few lines. Finds the address in her notes and runs to the post office. Not runs, exactly, but walks very fast. She's scared she'll change her mind. She buys an envelope and a stamp, writes the address on the envelope, and shoves it through the mail slot. She hears the letter drop. The box must be empty. No one writes letters on paper anymore. Only if there's no other option, and she has no other option. Then she slowly goes back. Home.

> *Dear sis!*
> *Stefans never talks about you, but not too long ago he said, "I know why you're waiting for Dina. I waited for you like that, too. You wait because you can't not wait." It's the most beautiful thing he's ever said to me.*

Sis! I need Stefans so much, so very much.

The city is just as pretty as when I left. It breathes to its own rhythm and sings people full of its sounds. The nights are cold, but the sun is still warm during the day. The old maple outside is already changing colors. At night I can hear the port, the ships and their setting out to sea. Or coming back.

Stefans and I drove to the seaside recently. The seagulls were crying, and I thought of Kristofs. All my thoughts turned to him. He is as big as the sea. As strong. "The river is a road to the sea," he told me once. But I'm so far from the river and that road. Sometimes, when I think of him, he narrows his eyes as the wind blows into them.

Dina! I'm going to go see Mom. I don't remember the last time I saw her. Four years?

Fucking time! It takes so much away.

Love you.

CHAPTER 11

Kristofs has almost steered the boat back into port when he gets the text from his sister: "Rute's gone."

What does that mean, gone? Where? Why? But he writes:

"Okay. How're the boys?"

"Good, growing. Call us sometime."

"I get home late."

Matilde doesn't write back.

"Hugs for the boys."

Port. The men unload their catch, exhausted. Bring their things to the warehouse, then head home. Kristofs is silent, but the men don't notice because they're not talkative right now either. That's how it is at night, all their jokes and laughter stay at sea and their wives welcome them home, tired and silent. No one waits up for Kristofs. He doesn't want anyone to. But now, Rute . . . He thinks about her all the time. What is that gray woman running away from? Because she *is* running away—Kristofs can see that. He's seen so many sea creatures run from the nets and traps. Eyes wide and frightened, their little brains thinking of

69

only one thing—escape. It's one of the most powerful instincts. And if they succeed, they disappear so fast you barely have time to register it. Rute has the same frightened eyes, with the same, sole thing on her mind—escape. And now she's gone.

Kristofs pours himself a whiskey and turns on the TV. He doesn't care what's on. He can't get Rute out of his mind. He remembers the time she was floating in the river, the seaweed winding around her body, her gray hair fanned out and swirling around her head like snakes.

He has the sudden desire to catch her in a net or a trap. And never let her go. So that she stops running, learns to stay in one place. And if necessary he'll anchor her down, like you do with pots and pans on the boat. You anchor everything on a boat, because anything can be lost at sea, get thrown overboard and washed away.

Kristofs pours himself another drink. The silence of the apartment makes him uncomfortable. There are always sounds at sea: the motor running, the waves lapping against the side of the boat, the wind. The silence in the apartment scares him. It's hard for him to fall asleep when it's this quiet. He starts to wonder if he shouldn't change boats. Transfer to a bigger one, one that comes back to port less often. So he'd be farther away from it all.

He dreams of Rute. She smiles and comes to him. Leans down to his ear and whispers:

"What are *you* running from?"

He wakes up.

—Kid, you need a woman! Gunārs jokes the following morning. You're getting too serious.

—That's life, Kristofs huffs.

—Princess, they don't live in the sea, stop staring out at it all the time, Māris chimes in.

—I'm watching the dolphins, stupid.

The other two men exchange glances and nod.

—Yep. A woman.

Toward evening Gunārs shouts that he's having a little get-together over the weekend, that Kristofs should come. Kristofs shouts back he'd rather hang out with the dolphins, but of course he goes. Even buys a new shirt for it. He brings flowers for Gunārs's wife. He likes Gunārs's wife. She reminds him of Matilde, looks for the good in everything and doesn't worry about tomorrow. Māris is there, with his girlfriend and son, and there's also an older Latvian couple, along with two young women from Latvia.

—Kid, you've got options, Gunārs whispers to him. They're both totally single.

—How do you know?

—I just know—look at their hands.

Kristofs looks, but Gunārs starts to laugh. Kristofs sees he was joking.

—Important thing is: there're no dolphins here. It'll be fine! Gunārs thumps him on the shoulder.

The night goes how it always does with expats: the introductions, then the talk about Latvia, which region each of them is from. The complaints about how low the wages back home are, how stupid the government is. As the night wears on the smokers start to go out for a cigarette more and more often. When the conversation turns more political, several of them all talk at once. And then Kristofs falls asleep.

He wakes up after the older couple has already gone home.

—Have a nice nap, princess? Māris pours Kristofs another drink.

—I'm good, Kristofs pushes the glass away.

A lock of hair from the young woman sitting next to him brushes his arm. Her hair is just as gray as Rute's. He takes the lock in his fingers, and the young woman looks at him with surprise. Then she smiles and raises her glass.

—Cheers!

Kristofs stares back at her, then gets up to leave.

—Captain! Where're you going? the men call after him, but he doesn't look back.

—Home, he grunts and carefully shuts the door behind him.

Kristofs spends his next day off sleeping on the couch. He feels kind of shitty. He remembers the way it felt when he first started going to sea. That was kind of shitty, too, until he got used to it. But now he's too used to it. Sometimes he sits down on the toilet at home and grips the sides. It takes him a second to remember the room isn't swaying. Other times he walks through the apartment, practically strangling his coffee mug in his hands. He forgets he can safely set it down on the table. The room isn't going to buck and roll and knock the mug over. These are the little things that live inside him. The things that make him happy. If only he didn't miss Lūkass. And Matilde, and the baby.

That night he gets in his car and drives and drives. Nowhere in particular, simply drives and looks out at the sleeping city. The streets are empty and peaceful.

The following morning on the boat, he's singing loudly and joyfully. Māris and Gunārs look at one another and grin. Everything is okay.

—If the captain is singing, it'll be a good day at sea. An old British saying, Māris claims.

—The Irish have one too: if the captain is singing, the dolphins will be happy, Gunārs jokes, and they all laugh.

Kristofs loves these men. He runs a good team, a team he can depend on.

—Latvians have one that's a bit different: if a crew talks too much about sayings, the captain makes them scrub the toilets, Kristofs quips and disappears into the wheelhouse.

CHAPTER 12

It's cold. Rute pulls her scarf tighter around herself as she stands at the prison gate. She's waiting there with several other women: an older one, two loud gypsies, and a very young girl. There's the jangling of keys, and then they follow the guard into the prison grounds. Rute doesn't want to look up, doesn't want to see the barbed wire and barred windows. She keeps her eyes on her shoes and walks behind the older woman. They turn in their belongings, fill out a million forms, show their passports, and consent to be searched. Rute is treated well; she isn't made to strip down and bend over, like she's read about. But regardless, she feels like a puppet. Like Matilde and Kristofs on their leashes. She grits her teeth—she has to get through this, she has to. Then she's led to a large room where the inmates sit at tables and talk to their visitors—a lounge, a café without coffee or flowers on the tables, and without customers in fancy footwear. The room smells of immense aching. The inmates' eyes are like those of chained-up dogs.

There she is. Mother. Her mother. Rute walks slowly over and sits down across from her. Her mother looks the same as before. Short hair sticking out in all directions, large wrinkles at the corners of her mouth—the kind all smokers have—her face pale. Her mother used to always be tan from all the time she spent outdoors. But here the sun is on the other side of the bars. Bars everywhere. Rute sees her mother is clenching her hands in an effort to keep them from shaking. Her mother's hands are beautiful, even when clenched like that; they're trembling like aspen leaves.

—Hi, Rute says softly.

—Sweetheart . . . I . . . I . . .

Her mother swallows back tears and more tears. She can't speak.

—How are you? Rute tries to help.

—Fine, everything's fine, her mother lies, because there's no way things can be fine in prison.

—They feeding you well? No one's hurting you?

—Fine, everything's fine, her mother repeats and keeps swallowing back tears.

Rute wants to take her mother by the hand, to soothe her, like people who soothe other people do. But they're mother and daughter. The daughter can't take the mother's hand here and soothe her. Here, Rute, the daughter, hurts. So much.

—How are you? Her mother has stopped gulping and smiles.

—Good, Rute answers.

—How's Stefans? You still together?

—Yes, Mom. Stefans is fine. We . . . Rute falls silent.

Mother and daughter don't know what to say to one another. There's a mountain of things to talk about, but no capability to do so.

—I went to Dad's place, by the river, the daughter says and the mother looks surprised.

—Did you see him?

—No, he's dead. He left me the house. Have you ever been there?

—I have, her mother sighs, that's where Dina was born.

Rute shrinks at the sound of the name. It's been ages since she's heard her mother say "Dina."

—Have you heard anything? her mother asks and starts gulping again.

—No, Rute shakes her head.

—I write her letters, her mother says, then jumps to her feet. I'll get them for you! Will you give them to her, if you see her?

But then her mother remembers she's in prison. That she can't just run off to get something.

—Mom, I don't know. Dina . . . I don't know. Rute takes a deep breath, her dry mouth hanging open. Dina's been gone for so long.

—Ten years and ninety-four days, her mother says.

Mother and daughter don't share their doubts with each other. The doubts sneak up unexpectedly, and they both drive them away. Dina is alive. Definitely. It's something to hold onto, the only way to go on living.

—I used to really like swimming in the river. Her mother doesn't want to talk about Dina anymore.

Rute nods.

—I'd pick sweet flag and whorled mint and put them in vases.

—Why did you leave Dad? Because he was the village idiot? Rute is suddenly bitter.

—I don't know. Something deep down . . . I was looking for something else. Something called to me . . . very strongly. So strong I couldn't fight it. It still calls to me, but now there's all *this*, her mother gestures with a hand.

Rute looks around. The older woman she'd been waiting with at the gate is at another table, reading to her adult daughter. Just reading to her. The daughter listens, and there is a tenderness there, seaweed wrapping and bringing them together. But the river between Rute and her mother is frozen, the ice is so thick the current can't shift it. The sun doesn't shine on their side of the river.

—I have to go now, Mom, Rute says when she can't take it anymore.

—Will you come back?

Rute nods. As a person to a person, or as a daughter to a mother? Will Rute come back? She stands abruptly and leaves her mother at the table, leaves quickly. Quickly, in order to hide from everyone. From her mother and father, from Dina . . .

That night, Stefans sees Rute's tear-stained face and asks what happened.

—Rute, please! Don't be so distant.

When Rute is hurting she shrinks deep into herself, dives down to the bottom of the river and into silence. But this time Stefans dives with her and shakes her by the shoulder, stays with her at the bottom, among the shards of clay and old bricks, among the perch and pike swimming past.

—I went to see my mom, she whispers, and then they both resurface.

—Oh! Stefans pulls her tightly to him.

—My mom writes letters to Dina . . . and she had no idea Dad had died, Rute murmurs.

—Dad? Stefans is confused because she hasn't told him about her father or the house by the river.

—My dad's dead. I never told you. It happened a while ago. But I never knew him, nor did you and . . .

—Rute? Why are you so far away from me?

—I don't know. I don't know, she whispers.

—Your mother and your sister . . . You're going to carry that with you forever, aren't you?

Rute nods.

—With me, in me. I don't know how to exist without it.

—When's the last time you laughed, Rute? he asks, and she thinks.

She tries to remember. Tries to hear what her laughter sounds like. And she hears it. Her laughter and Lūkass's. She can laugh with Lūkass. Then her mother and sister disappear somewhere.

Stefans gently traces a finger down her cheek. He used to do that back when they were both still very young and just getting to know one another.

She has never told him that she loves him.

CHAPTER 13

Olga comes over the following day. Wednesday. Olga has been coming every Wednesday for several years. First she goes over the apartment with a damp cloth, wiping down the shelves, windowsills, and cupboards; then she vacuums, deep-cleans, disappears into the bathroom, the half bath, the kitchen. When she gets to Rute's office the two of them usually have a tea break. In the beginning Rute felt self-conscious around Olga—self-conscious because someone else was cleaning her house. Rute used to go out on Wednesdays to avoid her. But Stefans didn't want Rute cleaning such a large apartment herself.

—Hah, and good thing, too! Olga smiles. I have work! I get paid well! She laughs, then wiggles her hips. And it's a great way to stay in shape!

She was a talker; a heartfelt and bright chatterbox. And so she and Rute began having tea together.

—Why the long face? Olga asks as she wheels the vacuum into the office.

—Hmm. Well. I went to see my mom yesterday.

—Ah yes, every time I see mine I want to launch the entire world to the moon! Olga laughs again and Rute wonders how she can do that so easily.

She wants to be able to do that, too.

—Mine's in prison, Rute says. I hadn't seen her in almost five years.

—How come? Is what she did so terrible that you don't want to see her?

Rute nervously drums her fingers on the table.

—I knew your mother was in prison, Olga says and sits down next to Rute. Make us some tea?

And Rute does. She boils water, pours loose-leaf herbal tea into the teapot. The smell of peppermint wafts up to her, and she thinks of the house by the river. She carries the teapot and two mugs back to her office.

Olga is sitting at the desk, gazing out the window.

—Did you grab the honey?

—Oops, forgot, Rute goes back to get it.

—While you were gone, Stefans's mother was here one day, yelling about your mother, too, Olga says when Rute returns to the office a second time. She was saying some nasty things.

—Like what? Rute wants to know.

Olga gives her a long look.

—Fine, I'll tell, but only because I also think you were awful to disappear like that. You can't toy with people that way. With Stefans.

Rute looks away. The chickens have come to roost—that's what Vladimirs used to say. Or had it been Igors? Rute can't remember the names of all her mother's men.

—She went on about how enough was enough, she wasn't going to just sit back and watch anymore. How she'd said nothing for so long, but no more. She told Stefans to think about what life would be like without you. Told him to find an easier woman. That's what she said. And how she was scared for him. You're the daughter of a convict, after all. And then she lay into him, wanted him to tell her what your mother had done to wind up in prison. Then she said that maybe your sister had done something bad, too, that's why she'd gone into hiding. And maybe you'd done the same—did he even know where you were?

Rute listens and feels like she is being slapped and slapped and slapped—and she keeps turning the other cheek to take it. The chickens have come to roost.

—She said she'd held her tongue when Stefans had first taken you in like some beggar off the street, but that enough was enough, she wasn't going to hold back anymore.

—I'm so sorry, Olga adds when she sees the blotchy red of Rute's cheeks.

—And what did Stefans say? Rute asks and covers her eyes with her hands.

—Nothing. And then his mother left and slammed the door. And then . . . he started to put your things in boxes.

Rute doesn't want that. She doesn't want to hurt Stefans. She wants to laugh and to live.

—Where were you all summer? Olga asks.

—My dad's house, by the river, Rute answers and then adds: I needed to . . .

—To what? Olga presses.

—I don't know . . . Rute admits.

—Don't do it again, okay? Olga wants her to promise, and she does.

Then they drink their tea and Olga talks about her kids, her husband—who has apparently lost his mind because he's decided, in his old age, to buy a boat.

—I hate cleaning fish! No boat and no fishing! Olga laughs again.

Then she takes the vacuum and disappears into the bed-room.

Dina!!!

Pain gives birth to pain, I know that now. A person who is hurt will always hurt others. A happy person will bring happiness. I don't know how to break free.

It gets dark so fast at night. The city is waiting for winter. Waiting to be snowed under, snowed in, to look white and pure. I don't like that kind of snow. It masks reality.

But is reality just pain?

Is there a school for laughter? If there was I think I'd like to sign up.

Dina! Our mother's in prison. I haven't told anyone why. Sometimes I wonder: what would I tell my kids, if I had any? That their grandma is in prison because she accidentally killed her fiancé? Or partner, whatever you want to call him. I don't even know his name. Our mother is a murderer. Those are loud and painful words.

It was an accident, Dina, you have to know that. It was self-defense gone wrong. Dina, how am I going to explain all of this when you come back?

It's probably cold and dark at Dad's house. The river runs its course, naked. The books in the house shiver and try to warm each other up.

Dina, I wrote an article for a magazine. About curtains! Stefans says I have a gift for writing. That I should write more—even if it's just about curtains. And so I did. About the light-blocking kind, thin curtains, curtain pulls, and how to clean them all. I wrote and thought about the curtains at Dad's house. The sun-yellow ones Matilde and Kristofs gave me. It's not like I don't have anything else to do—I have a number of translating jobs—but writing for yourself is completely different. Stefans laughed about my article: what was I going to write about next? Pans?

If Stefans is my home, then what's back there, at the house by the river? What's calling me back there?

Dina, I love you so, so much.

CHAPTER 14

Rute and Stefans go see a therapist together, to get Rute's laughter back. The therapist, Aiga, has Rute and Stefans start with an icebreaker; they have to ask each other ten questions. Rute goes first.

—What's your name?

—Stefans.

Rute thinks, but doesn't know what else to ask.

—What's your favorite color?

—Green.

—Your favorite food?

—Ice cream.

—What do you like to do?

—My wife.

Rute blushes a deep red and glances at Aiga, who smiles.

—What else?

—Cook.

—What did you want to be when you grew up?

—A chef.

—Why aren't you one?

—No one in my family becomes a chef. We all wind up in business and strategy, or on management boards.

—Do you want to quit?

—It's not that easy. I don't know, I haven't thought about it.

—How old are you?

—Thirty-seven.

—What's your favorite movie?

—*Star Wars*, obviously. Like all guys.

It's strange, asking questions to the person you spend the most time with, the person you're closest to. To ask and to hear. To listen.

—Now it's your turn, Stefans, Aiga says.

Stefans looks intently at Rute.

—What's your name?

—Rute.

—Where were you this summer?

Rute doesn't reply and shoots the therapist a scared look.

—I don't want to.

—You don't have to. But it'll make getting to know each other harder.

—We already know each other, Rute insists.

—Really? Aiga says calmly.

—What's your favorite color?

—Light blue.

—Where were you this summer?

—Stefans, stop . . .

—I want to know you.

—I can't right now.

A silence falls over them. Pain on both their faces, even though they came here to find laughter.

—What's your favorite food?

Rute starts to cry. She suddenly doesn't know what her favorite food is, doesn't know what foods she likes, what scents she likes, or where she was this summer. Nor does she want to know the answer to any of it.

Dear sis!

We didn't find my laughter, and I don't know if I'll keep looking for it. Stefans isn't pressuring me, but keeps saying that he wants to get to know me, wants us to be close. I don't know, I don't know . . .

Isn't it strange? I don't know what foods I like, but I remember what you like. Halva. Nettle soup. Crusty bread with butter.

I remember what you were wearing the last time we saw each other.

Jeans, heavy black boots, a gray, thick-knit sweater. A black coat and moss-green scarf. That's what you looked like when you left my place to go back to yours. I remember it was really windy that day. I didn't walk you out.

I didn't.

Walk.

You.

Out.

I didn't know it would be the last time I'd see you. I keep thinking and asking myself if everything would have been different if I'd walked you to the bus stop. Even partway.

Dina . . .

CHAPTER 15

Stefans had wine at the office, so he can't take the car home. The city is full of snow and he decides to walk. Millions of little lights glimmer in the city's trees. People stand looking at them, their heads tilted back, mouths open in wonder. Stefans remembers how his mother never let him stand around with his mouth gaping open like that.

—A crow'll shit in there, she'd said, and he had believed her.

There were a lot of mean things crows could do: shit in your mouth, steal your candy, peck you in the ass, even rip out your hair. That's why Stefans didn't like crows for a long time. He still doesn't really like them to this day, even though he knows now that the crows of his childhood were like the Tooth Fairy or Easter Bunny. But those stories stay with you. "Parents should think before they talk," he muses.

He walks through the tunnel and turns down a small side street. He's no longer surrounded by millions of little lights, and a sense of dread washes over him.

Then someone shoves him. Stefans drops to one knee and takes a punch to the back. He's scared. He curls up into a ball and feels the contact of heavy boots. Against his face, his stomach, his legs. He shields himself with his hands, and his hands take the brunt of the attack. He tastes blood and thinks about his teeth. He's terrified of the dentist. Terrified of the needles and the drills. Terrified of the pain.

—I hate these rich fuckers! he hears one of the boots say.

Then they empty his pockets. One more kick to the back, and the boots leave. Stefans hears a tram drive by in the distance. He raises his head and sees a stop on the opposite side of the street. It's deserted. He drags himself over to it and sits down. His body hurts and his clothes reek. What a rich pussy he is. Why didn't he put up a struggle? Fight back? Does he even know how to throw a punch? Has he ever been in a fight, gotten a black eye?

When he unlocks the door, Rute is in the kitchen. She's baking something—a sweet scent wafts through the apartment. Cinnamon, butter, sugar . . .

Rute comes to greet him, a floral apron around her waist. A sprinkle of flour in her gray hair. And on her cheek. She probably tried to push her hair back from her face, and the flour from her hand stayed behind.

Stefans stands and watches her. She flinches when she sees the blood seeping from her husband's eyebrow. Sees his dirty coat and bruised hands.

—I have to pee, Stefans says and goes to the bathroom.

His entire body is shaking. He unzips his fly and takes out his penis with trembling hands. Everything is shaking, he can't pee. He just stands and stands. Then Rute comes into the bathroom and hugs him from behind. He starts to cry, his penis still in his hands.

—I can't pee, he tells her, and she hugs him tighter.

The sweet scent is in the bathroom now as well. Stefans takes slow breaths. He closes his eyes. Feels Rute's strength and is amazed at it. She's so fragile, but when she needs to she carries all the strength of the world in her. She's home, Stefans realizes then, and a strong and warm stream empties into the toilet. Rute holds him, doesn't let go until he's finished peeing. Then she helps him undress. Gets some hydrogen peroxide to clean his wounds. Fills the bath, helps him get in. Sits on the edge of the tub and swirls her hand in the water.

Stefans thinks about his cowardice, his fear.

—Rute, this here is our little world . . . Sometimes I forget things are different out there.

—What's different? Rute asks.

—Out there you get beat and bitten. It's hard to survive. Fuckers . . . fuckers . . . I should be stronger . . .

Rute smiles, picks up a bath sponge and washes his shoulders, arms.

—You are, she says, but Stefans sneers.

—I'm a pussy.

Rute gets a small pair of scissors and trims his fingernails.

—I like pussies, she says, and he laughs.

Then he grimaces because it hurts his stomach. His body has been kicked in and around too much.

—They took my phone. My wallet.

Rute is silent, but then says sternly:

—You're alive and that's what matters.

—Rute, you don't get it . . . I cried!

—And?

—I'm not supposed to cry.

—Because?

Stefans stands and gets out of the tub. Rute wraps a warm towel around him.

—Are you going to go to the police?

—No, it's not worth it, muggings are a dime a dozen.

—True, she says, they are.

Then she makes a strong pot of herbal tea.

—Want to watch an old movie?

—Sure, he says and curls up on the couch with a quiet moan.

Rute can see he's in more pain than he's letting on. The slightest movement and he grits his teeth.

—Maybe we should go to the hospital?

—Maybe we can play doctor right here at home? Stefans jokes, and she wants to swat at him but catches herself.

He doesn't see much of the movie. He falls asleep, and in his dream he is in the glow of millions of small bright lights in the trees. Then the lights flap their wings and turn into gray crows that fly in circles around him. Then he wakes up.

CHAPTER 16

Rute spends all winter reading about rivers. Tenderizes meat for dinner and reads about rivers. Folds the clean laundry and reads about rivers. Puts on red lipstick and reads about rivers.

Smaller rivers are called streams . . .

Is Rute's river a stream?

An old river is a river with a slower current and lower erosion rate . . .

Floods are a natural part of a river's annual cycle . . .

She comes home from the theater and reads about rivers.

From a security standpoint, it was historically more convenient to place important settlements not directly on the seashore, where they were subject to ambush from the sea, but to place them along the river not far from the estuary . . .

Then she goes to the couch and sinks to her knees in front of Stefans. With a gentle and moist mouth bites his hand. Licks his finger and climbs into his lap. They have their own rhythm. They've lived together for so long, have slept with one another for so long, sleep inside one another. Their fingers have been inside one another, their tongues and their limbs. They have encompassed one another, bruised and scratched. Lost and found. They have their own ongoing rhythm. At times louder, quieter at others. Rute has seen them. Watched them in mirrors. Met the eyes of Stefans's reflection, when he's on top of her, inside of her and outside of her. When he licks the tip of his finger and traces her nipple with it. She's seen herself go down on him, pick a pubic hair out of her mouth, and clench his head between her knees. She has seen both of them, and he has seen both of them.

They have their own rhythm. Their scent. Stefans's ejaculate on the couch.

—We'll get a new one, he laughs, and Rute is happy.

The next morning, after Stefans has already left for work, Rute gets a text from Matilda. The old willow has fallen onto the roof of the house. Rute tosses a toothbrush into a bag, along with toothpaste, a clean pair of socks and panties, face cream, a water bottle, and her phone. Then she rushes to the bus depot. The city is waiting for spring. It's rained since the last snow, leaving a few sad, dirty piles of snow along the streets. Piles for dogs to shit in and kids to jump into. Their moms scold them and pull them away. Rute passes a café window and spots a couch inside. She remembers yesterday and smiles. Stefans! She stands on the sidewalk, thinking. Stefans. Stefans. Stefans . . . Then she goes back to the apartment and writes him a note, leaves it on the kitchen table.

The bus from Riga to Upesciems runs infrequently. Rute grows so cold while she waits that her lips turn blue. She reads the signs on the bus depot's walls. Why can't you feed the birds? Why can't you smoke, even though everyone smokes? If they smoke anyway, she should be able to feed the birds. Is feeding the birds worse than smoking?

When Rute arrives at the house, dusk is starting to settle. She stands in the yard for some time looking at the house, at the old willow on the roof. Only one of the branches has broken off, but it's a giant one. It had wanted to fall next to the house, but the house had moved closer. Now the branch lies across the roof, and there's a visible hole. An old house, an old willow, and an old Rute with her old stories. She goes into the kitchen, then into the bedroom and the spare room. Water is leaking from the ceiling. She places a bucket under the dripping water and returns to the kitchen. Her footsteps are heavy as she goes to get firewood. She tears off splinters for kindling and tears her hands apart—just like that first time. Then she runs to the river. It's dark again, with dried out reeds lining its banks. The old dock is almost entirely submerged, the poles that hold it up the only visible part. Rute sinks her hands into the cold water. Her heart is as freezing as the river today, icicles in her veins.

Then Rute goes to Matilde's house. Scolds herself for not bringing something for Lūkass and Niklāvs. But Lūkass doesn't need a gift. He sees Rute and races over to her so fast that knocks over little Niklāvs, who is unsteady on his feet as it is. Niklāvs falls and starts to cry. Matilde scoops him up with a smile. Lūkass clings to Rute.

—You came! He shouts joyfully.

—I came, Rute smiles at him.

—Did you see the tree on your house?

—I did, Rute nods.

Matilde joins them and hugs Rute tightly.

—Come in! You're frozen.

—Yeah, a bit, Rute shivers.

—Once your lips turn blue you're past "a bit," she laughs with her big teeth.

Matilde takes Rute inside. She takes two glasses from the cupboard and pours each of them some black currant Balzams. Rute takes a sip and heat courses immediately through her body.

—It's strong.

—It is, Matilde agrees. How's the house? The roof?

—There's a hole. And a leak, Rute says.

—Are you going to fix it? Matilde asks, and Rute looks at her with surprise.

—Fix it? Of course, I have to.

—It's an old house, Matilde adds carefully.

—You don't think it's worth it? Rute is confused.

Matilde shrugs and pours each of them another glass of Balzams. Lūkass climbs into Rute's lap and shoves a cookie into her mouth.

—Lūkass, be nice! Matilde scolds him.

—I am! He answers resolutely and keeps feeding her.

—Lūkass, how are you? Rute asks the boy and squeezes him tightly.

—Great! I have rabbits!

—You have rabbits? You guys have rabbits? Rute turns to Matilde.

—Yes, a few. The boys wanted a pet, Matilde laughs again.

—Want to see them? Lūkass asks.

—I do!

—Lūkass, it's dark out, Matilde says, but Lūkass has a lantern and he and Rute are already putting their boots on.

Outside is incredibly dark. They go behind the house, and there against the back wall are the rabbit hutches.

—Kristofs made them! Lūkass brags about both.

Very nice! The rabbits see the lamplight, hear their voices, and come to the wire mesh to meet them. The rabbits sniff their visitors with velvet noses, twitch their whiskers. Lūkass slides a finger carefully through the mesh and ruffles a rabbit's neck.

—Want to touch one? He asks Rute and she nods.

—Just watch your finger! Sometimes the rabbits think they're carrots, Lūkass adds, and then Rute reaches in to touch a spotted white rabbit.

—They're beautiful, Rute breathes.

—Yeah.

They stay with the rabbits for some time, but then they hear Matilde calling and head back inside.

—Matilde, they're beautiful!

—And not too messy. Only these tiny pellets, Matilda laughs and adds, what matters is that the boys like them.

—Matilde, you're a good mom, Rute says.

—If you say so.

After the boys go to bed, Rute tells Matilde everything.

About Stefans.

—You're married?

About her mother, prison, the murder.

—Has she been in there long?

And about the hardest part. About Dina.

—Do you think she'll come back?

Rute doesn't know, but wants to know. Really, really wants to.

—Dina is older than me, Rute talks, but now she's younger. Does that make sense? She disappeared when I was twenty-six and she was twenty-nine. Now I'm thirty-six, but she's still twenty-nine. I don't know the older her. I don't know if she still sounds like herself or if she looks the same.

—Rute, I don't know what to say.

—She's been gone for ten years. According to the law I can now have her officially declared dead. Inherit her assets, social security. But I don't even know if Dina owned anything. I don't think she did. And how can I be sure she's actually dead? Did someone see the body? What would you do?

—I . . . I don't know.

—Me either. Rute shakes her head glumly.

—Maybe stay with us? Matilde offers when Rute gets ready to leave.

—No, it'll be fine, Rute assures her. I want to be there.

Matilde sends her off with provisions: a bag with some cucumbers and bread, some cookies and a packet of coffee. Then she presses Lūkass's lantern into her hands.

—Thank you, Rute hugs her.

Matilde stands watching the small ray of light grow weaker and weaker, until the dark fog of the river floods up over everything.

My dearest sister!

I'm trying to decide what to do with the house. It's super old, and now there's a hole in the roof. The old willow fell on it.

Do you want to see the house? If you knew it was here, would you come back?

Dina, I saw you one day. You were walking pretty fast down Elizabete Street. I called to you, but you kept walking. Then I ran after you and grabbed your shoulder. You turned and then it wasn't you anymore. I apologized to this stranger and hurried away.

Dina, what if you're actually dead? Are you dead???? How did you die? Why?????? Why is it easier for me to think of you as alive?

But who else can I write to? How could I live and not write?

What happens to a sister if her sister is dead?

Love you. Miss you. Begging you.

CHAPTER 17

Rute wakes at sunrise. The yellow curtains hadn't been pulled shut. She crawls out from under the blanket, where she slept fully clothed. After she has some coffee she goes down to the river. She spots something strange by the dock. The air is full of the strange thing. The river doesn't smell like a river. The wind carries the stench off the water. Rute wrinkles her nose and goes closer.

A wild boar is snagged between the dock posts. A rotting, putrid wild boar. It must've fallen through the ice in the winter and now the spring current has dredged it up. It's been pecked at by birds and saturated by water. Rute looks around for a large branch. Then she runs up to the shed and comes back with an old rake. She jabs the boar until the dock posts release it and it is carried further downstream.

Rute crouches by the river's edge and thinks about dying. About Dina. About the boar. Death seems to be as inevitable as life. Rute's legs have fallen asleep from the prolonged crouching, and she's about to get up when someone crouches next to her. Stefans! He found her!

They sit in silence and watch the river. The sun warms their backs. Rute feels so good when he's next to her. So safe.

—What's your name? Stefans asks and Rute smiles.

—Rute. She recognizes the game, and she'll play it.

—What're you doing here?

—Staring at the river. And the wild boar.

—Wild boar? Stefans suddenly looks around them, frantic.

—No, Rute laughs. It was in the river, but it's gone now.

—That's your house?

—No, my dad's

—Who's your dad?

—Jūle. Jūlijs. He's dead. I never met him, Rute smiles sadly.

—Why is there a branch on the roof?

—The tree is old. And the house is old.

Rute thinks for a moment.

—I don't know what to do.

—Can I help? Once you do know?

—Yes.

Rute takes his hand.

—Let's get up, I can't feel my legs.

They go inside hand in hand. She shows him everything and tells him as much as she knows, which isn't much. As they sit and eat the cucumbers and bread from Matilde, Stefans starts the game again.

—What's your name?

—Rute.

—Are you going to stay here?

—No, no.

—Where will you go?

—Home. To my husband.

—Oh, you have a husband?

—Yes, one, she laughs.

—That's a lot. But is it enough?

Rute is silent.

—The curtains are nice, Stefans gestures to them.

—They are, the neighbors got them for me.

—There's something else out here besides wild boar?

—Yes, Matilde, and her two boys. Niklāvs and Lūkass. She has a brother, too, Kristofs, but he lives at sea and rarely visits.

—Sounds nice.

—To live at sea?

—No, that you didn't spend the summer completely alone.

Then they go outside. Stefans takes a look at the willow and thinks about what to do about the roof. They both look around the shed and at Rute's dahlia garden, which won't grow anymore because she forgot about them. She should have dug up the bulbs, stored them over the winter. She shows him a crow's nest and walks the old bicycle over to him. Stefans rides it around, laughing—it's been ages since he's ridden a bike. Then Rute teaches him how to light the stovetop. Shows him how to draw water from the well. Then she reads to him from one of Jūle's books. They're so, so close, tucked in under the old blankets.

When they leave for home later that night, Rute rests her hand on Stefans's knee.

—It can be enough, she says, and Stefans smiles in the dark.

CHAPTER 18

Her mother has asked Rute many times to come visit, but she hasn't agreed to until now.

—Thank you for coming, her mother says as Rute sits down across from her.

—I didn't have the time, Rute lies awkwardly.

—I know, I know, I'm busy too,

Rute gives a pained smile and bites back:

—Oh? What're you up to?

Her mother takes it and withstands it. Absorbs the barb.

—I'm trying to balance work with my studies. We have jobs here: sewing dresses for the military, her mother jokes.

—What are you studying?

—Culinary arts. I want to work when I get out.

—Okay, Rute says slowly.

—I've never really worked before . . .

They fall silent.

—How are you? Her mother asks and Rute retreats into herself.

She doesn't want to talk about it, and her mother can tell.

—Tell me! Her mother begs.

Rute doesn't like it when she begs. Rute tells her about the branch that fell on the roof of the river house. And about Stefan's mugging. About the rabbits and the wild boar. Nothing more.

—Are you not sleeping? Her mother suddenly asks. You have rings under your eyes.

—Yeah, Rute sighs.

—Know what's strange? Prison is the first place I've ever slept a deep sleep. Sleep on the outside was always disjointed, I'd wake up a lot. Like I was afraid to be asleep. But it's safe here . . . my head hits my pillow at night and next thing I know it's morning.

—I don't think I'm afraid of anyone, Rute says, then adds: Anymore.

Another barb. Her mother withstands that one as well.

—Say hi to Stefans for me? Her mother asks when Rute gets up to leave.

—I will.

—I've met someone, her mother says and, when she sees Rute's confusion, continues dreamily: Well, we haven't met in person. We've been writing to each other. He has to wait just a little bit longer . . .

Rute stands outside the prison gate for some time. Then she heads to the tram stop. A young man on an electric scooter zooms past. He's carrying a large bag of potatoes. Rute smiles and thinks of when she and Kristofs planted potatoes for Matilde.

Dina!

When mom talked about sleeping poorly, it was the first time I felt like she was being a mother. For a second it seemed like that river was thawing. But then she told me she's met someone. He's in the men's prison.

Dina!

She's still picking her way through those same land-mines. She's still a little girl.

Love you.

CHAPTER 19

Kristofs nails down the last board and the fencing for the rabbits is done. He and Lūkass take the rabbits out of their cages and set them on the green grass. At first the rabbits shrink into themselves and sniff the air cautiously. Then they begin to slowly hop around and explore their new boundaries.

Kristofs ruffles Lūkass's hair.

—Good?

—Yesssssss! The boy whoops.

They watch the rabbits a bit more and then Kristofs goes inside. Lūkass stays in the yard. Matilde is peeling carrots for lunch.

—For the rabbits? Kristofs smiles.

—For us. It's easier if *everyone* eats the same thing, she jokes, and they both laugh.

—Matilde? Give me Rute's number.

—Why?

—I want to see her.

Matilde's hands go still and a worry line flashes across her forehead.

—Kristofs, she's married.

Somewhere deep down the wind is knocked out of him. But he keeps it together, he's spent his entire life keeping it together.

—So? I just want to see her.

Matilde thinks feverishly. Kristofs is her brother. Rute is her friend. Brother. If she could, she would do whatever it took to keep her brother from ever getting hurt again. But she can't do that, so she gives him Rute's phone number.

Kristofs wants to call Rute that night, but doesn't. Instead he thinks about her eyes. Rute's eyes are Jūle's eyes. Full of old stories. He thinks about Jūle. How he'd go to his house to listen to him read. How together they'd tighten screws and pound nails. Jūle was his closest male person—that's what their grandma used to say and she never stopped Kristofs from visiting him. Kristofs remembers driving Jūle to the doctor because of the pain in his stomach.

—Your stomach is a bit lower than that, Kristofs had said, seeing that Jūle's hand was resting on his heart.

Then Jūle brought his hand lower, but the pain in his heart stayed where it was. Jūle had wanted to protect Kristofs even then, giant that he'd grown up to be.

—Probably just ate something bad, Jūle said.

Then there was the day Kristofs found Jūle at home on the floor. The same way he'd once found his grandma. Kristofs remembers Jūle's eyes as he lay there on the ground. Glassy eyes, like the ones used for dolls. Rute has the same eyes, except that hers are alive. Rute's eyes look at him and tease him. Kristofs hears the cries of gulls. He presses his hands over his ears but he can still hear them. Crying and crying. Kristofs can't escape the gulls anymore. They live inside him, claw at him and shriek their horrible cry.

Kristofs needs some air. He throws on his jacket and runs out of the house. Goes down to the river and then along the fishermen's path to Rute's house. Jūle's house. Rute still hasn't fixed the roof; the branch lies where it fell. Kristofs circles the house. Tries the door. Looks through the window at the emptiness inside. A familiar emptiness.

Again a gull cries within him. Spreads and flaps its wings. Inside. Now Jūle and little Kristofs are in there as well. Jūle teaching Kristofs to light a fire. Jūle showing him how to cook the fish they've caught. Jūle lighting dry leaves and blowing on the fire to stoke it. More and more, until the fire comes to life.

Kristofs knows how to light a fire. Knows how to gather up old, dried grasses, knows how to light a match. There's a box in the shed, always has been.

Kristofs blows fire into Rute's house. There, where the gull cries. The gull is spooked by the fire and tries to get away. It's never cried this shrilly before.

Let that cry burn up, along with its outspread wings, stop once and for all!

Matilde knows, but says nothing. She only goes to Rute's house after Kristofs has returned to sea. The house is surrounded by blackened ruins. The chimney looks like it's rising right up out of the ground. The air still smells of smoke. Like bonfire and seared fish. Matilde stands by the house and thinks. Remembers the fear . . . She and the boys had stood by their house praying to god that the firefighters would put out the flames. Prayed for god to control the wind so it wouldn't carry the fire to her house.

Matilde remembers how Rute had cried. Wailed like an animal and sobbed:

All of it's dead, everything I wouldn't let die . . .

Time to head back. The boys will wake soon. Matilde will make them pancakes. Yes. The three of them will sit at the kitchen table and eat with their hands. Then Lūkass will run to feed his rabbits, and after that they'll all go outside. She'll sit in the hammock and read a book. It's been so long since she's read a book. Well. Time to go.

Dear sis!

The river house burned down, so you'll never get to see it. Stefans said he'd build me a new one, but I don't know. He said he'd dig me a new river, too, if need be, but I don't think it's needed. I'm happy with what I have. I have. I have so very much. It's enough.

I wrote a new article for a magazine. No, not about pans. I wrote about rivers. About big ones, fast ones, and the small ones we call streams. I wrote about how a river tastes. About river water in your mouth, about the fish in the river and the rushes.

Sis!

I had you declared officially deceased. They said they were sorry they couldn't find you. I said there was still plenty of time, and they held their heads down. Then Stefans held me. Rocked me and rocked me. Rocked me into living.

Sis! I love him. I said it to him one day.

Sis!

We'll see each other again. I'm the one with the gray hair and bony ass. I'll be very, very old. I won't have my dentures in, so I'll probably look pretty strange.

But not yet. Not now. Right now I'm going to live life.

Love you.

Dina's missing person flyer

Dina and Rute as teenagers

Baby Rute and her mother

Matilde, grade 12

Jūle with a young Kristofs

Kristofs's fishing boat

The prison

Rute

Lūkass and his rabbits

Rute and Stefans

Laura Vinogradova (1984) is the author of two collections of short stories (*exhalations* and *Bear Hill*), and the novels *The River* (2020) and *Crows* (2024). *The River*, which has been translated into several languages, was shortlisted for the 2020 Latvian Literature Award and received a 2021 EU Prize for Literature.

Kaija Straumanis is an award-winning translator from the Latvian. She has translated works by Inga Gaile, Zigmunds Skujiņš, Jānis Joņevs, and Gundega Repše, among others. Her translation of Jānis Joņevs's *Doom 94* was the recipient of the 2019 Lillian Fairchild Memorial Award, and she received a 2020 NEA Translation Fellowship for her work on *Forest Daughters*, ed. Sanita Reinsone.